MORE THAN WE LOVED

REBECCA STONE

All rights reserved. No part of this book may be reproduced in any form or by any electronic means, including information storage and retrieval systems, without permission in writing from the author, except by a reviewer who may quote brief passages in review.

This is a work of fiction. Any resemblance to actual persons, living or dead, events, or locales is entirely coincidental. Any trademarks, service marks, product names, or named features are assumed to be the property of their respective owners, and are used only for reference. There is
no implied endorsement if any of these terms are used.

Copyright © 2021 by Rebecca Stone
All rights reserved.
Cover design by Rebecca Stone
ISBN

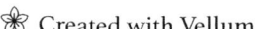 Created with Vellum

1

"I love you, Jules."

Warmth spread through Julie even as Anthony's rich voice shook across the video call, cutting in and out amidst a bad connection and background whooping and hollering. The night they'd finally decided to move forward — together — felt so far away, a lucid dream. Over the past seven or eight months, hearing those words from his lips was something she'd never gotten used to. Julie didn't think she ever would.

"I love you too, Anthony." Blowing him a kiss, Julie dallied with ending the call. He usually pulled the trigger. Having been on tour since May, Anthony had places to go and people to meet. But he always made time to connect with her every day, whether it was a sweet good morning text or a short video call.

Julie pulled her sweater close around her. The November chill was stronger in his absence. She tried to hold onto the feel of his body against hers, muscled and warm. The way his hands caressed her skin, grazing every valley, grasping every mountain with need. The way those hands — with the help of his silky tongue, his beautiful cock — tended to the garden between her legs with intricate care. She sighed and closed her laptop. Chewed her lower lip, listening to the silence of her apartment. She moved into the three bedroom apartment in April, a few weeks after viewing it. Centered in the West Village, she loved the cozy feel of hardwood floors and crown molding as much as the location itself. It helped that the noise from the popular MacDougal Street didn't permeate the pre-war walls, creating a cocoon of silence that bordered on oppressive. Julie understood why her best friend Ella had gotten a cat as soon as she lived on her own.

But Julie had bigger plans, if they'd actually come through.

She left the small office, stopping before the closed door at the end of the hallway. The painted white solid pine door stared at her, reminiscent of the door in her childhood home. The door that scared her from remembering her deceased little sister, Hannah. Julie had stared at that door in her parent's house for years, either grasping the handle only to walk away, or just walking right past it as if the fatal car accident in which Julie had been driving hadn't happened. It didn't help that her mom had kept the room exactly the same for over ten years. Hannah's smell lingered on her bedding, her smile haunting in the pictures of her and her friends adorning the walls.

This new door was different. Julie knew that, intellectually. Left closed, it reminded her of how far she'd come. Left open, it reminded her of where she wanted to go.

Grasping the crystal knob, she turned and pushed the door open. Dusk filled the white room, the new-paint smell finally fading away. Two windows leading to a fire escape greeted her, the dark headboard of a full bed pressed against the window in the far corner, adorned with an array of stuffed animals. A nightstand and a desk stood before the second window, a large closet across from the foot of the bed. A beginner guitar stood in a stand beside a low bookshelf filled with everything from books for toddlers to How To's for kids. Everything was neutral, beige and white and black. A clean slate for a child to leave their mark. Their personality.

She'd begun the foster parent certification in June, shortly after Anthony had left for the summer festival tour with his band, Eternal Youths. The summer tour was followed by a fall support tour for Imagine Dragons, which he was due back from in a little over a week.

Julie walked around the open space, trailing her fingers along the bedspread. After volunteering at an orphanage in India in February and coming home to work the nonprofit branch — Wings — of her best friends' company, she'd wanted nothing more than to help kids. She finally felt like she'd found her calling, and every step she took to realize that dream had been easy. When she received her first paycheck as the CEO of the nonprofit and signed the lease on her new apartment, Julie knew it was time to fill the holes in her life with people. She applied to foster and took the classes. She made one of the three bedrooms in her apartment as kid-friendly and neutral as possible, open to whomever would arrive at her doorstep.

But she hadn't told Anthony. The guilt gnawed at her as she closed the door behind her, heading past the bathroom and her office, down the narrow hallway to the spacious living room and attached kitchen, her own bedroom right beside it. Julie hadn't told him. She pulled down her favorite lavender tea, going over the promise she'd made to herself when she first applied.

She'd only tell him if she got the call a child would be arriving.

That call never came, and she'd managed to convince herself that he didn't need to know until it did. They'd been on and off for three years — and then he'd taken off on tour. As much as Julie wanted to believe the feeling in her bones that he was her home, that every time he proclaimed his love for her it meant he wouldn't go anywhere, she couldn't allow herself to trust that just yet.

Couldn't allow herself to trust that once he knew she wanted to foster a child, he wouldn't leave.

2

One week.

One more week and he could hold the love of his life in his arms.

Anthony looked around the tour bus and ran his hands through his hair, barely noticing the ridge of the scar on his scalp. The reminder of the accident two years ago that changed his life. His drunk ass had finally gotten sober, and it only took a life-threatening car accident, brain trauma, broken limbs, and drug rehab to do it. Oh, and being babysat by Julie while the rest of the band went on tour last year so he could heal.

But that babysitting had led him to acknowledge that, without a doubt, she was the only one for him.

After they'd built their friendship and had one amazing night together, she ended things last summer and took off for five or six months to "find herself." Anthony had tried to move on. But no one could compete with the way her smile warmed him, the way she knew his innermost secrets and carried them as her own, the way she pushed and tested him to be better than he was. Anthony briefly thought of Ruby Delacey, the gap-toothed, curly-haired woman he'd had a short fling with in January and February. His cousin Gideon and Gideon's fiancée Ella had hosted a New Year's party where Anthony met Ruby, not knowing she was Julie and Ella's a coworker.

He'd tried to ease himself from Julie, but when the curvaceous blonde came back to New York City, all hope flew out the window.

"Hey, Ant." Gideon came up beside him.

"Hey." Anthony scooted on the couch, making room for his cousin. After Anthony found a box in his dad's closet that contained incriminating evidence of an affair with Gideon's widowed mom, it was hard to be in the same room alone. Gideon had wanted to hash it out with his mom and uncle before the tour while Anthony had pushed for waiting until after. He'd won out. Going on tour with his dad —

who was also the band's manager — would be hard enough with the cold shoulder Anthony had gotten after reconnecting with his estranged mom.

Not that that hadn't been disastrous in its own right.

Anthony sighed, crossing his arms and letting his legs splay out.

"Same," Gideon said. "Ready to be home, in a real bed, and off this fucking bus. I swear if I have to listen anymore to Max go on about designer hats and Lucas snore I'm going to lose my shit."

Anthony laughed. Their saxophonist was desperately missing his hat collection and their drummer's nighttime melodies traveled the length of the bus every night. Anthony had no doubt this would be Eternal Youths' first and last tour with Imagine Dragons, solely because of that.

The passing streetlights flickered through the shared tour bus as they made their way to the next city — somewhere in the south, Atlanta maybe. Time and place was illogical after spending so many months on the road. Anthony could hear the murmured voices of his dad, Imagine Dragons' manager Matthew and their publicist Isaac, and Eternal Youths' publicist and Gideon's fiancée, Ella, in the dining section towards the back of the bus. Most of the band members were in their bunks, with the exception of Ryan, Eternal Youths' bassist, who sat at a table with his laptop and headphones, typing away.

"How are you feeling?" Gideon's voice cut through Anthony's thoughts of being in such close quarters with so many people for so long.

Anthony shrugged. "Fine. I missed the tour last year, so it's been nice to go along for the ride. It's been fun, opening for Imagine Dragons. I know there was some contention before about touring with them or Arctic Monkeys, but I think this was the right move."

"Sure, sure, I meant more about... How are you feeling about going back to New York City?"

How do you feel about going back to Julie?

Anthony knew what his cousin was really asking.

"You know I can't fucking wait, man. Why?"

Gideon shrugged. "Just checking. I know you and Julie had just gotten together before you left, and now you've been gone for so long. It'd be understandable if you were nervous and shit."

"Nah, she was gone for just as long last year and it only made us realize how much we wanted each other. It'll be nice to try the couple thing out for real this time." Anthony stood and stretched, trying to ignore the tightness in his chest as he walked to his bunk. "I'm calling it a night, see you tomorrow."

3

Across the office, Julie watched Ruby Delacey at her desk, typing away on her laptop. Julie turned back to her mug on the kitchen counter, pulling the steeped tea bag. She sat down at her own desk in front of the large windows. Ella was on her left, Rachel on her right. Julie's two best friends had founded Maven Media, a publicity company for the arts with a specialty in crisis management. They'd put Julie in charge of their nonprofit branch, Wings, to help at-risk women and children.

But from her position centered at the back of the office, Julie couldn't help being distracted by Ruby. The freckled beauty with a shock of red curly hair and her fling with Anthony. Granted, he and Julie weren't even speaking at the time. And maybe Julie had been literally halfway around the world, volunteering in India. But there was something about seeing the woman Anthony had a fling with.

Every. Single. Day.

Julie sighed, drawing her attention back to her laptop. Focus. She needed to focus. The dream was to apply for 501(c) status and tax exemptions by the end of the year. Two months wasn't an impossible deadline, but it was tight. Their lawyers were preparing to file for the Employer Identification Number with the IRS while they waited on the incorporation approval of Wings. They'd taken awhile to build a Board of Directors; Julie sat as the President and Maven Media's human resources manager Priya Somari sat as the Secretary. Ben, Rachel's roommate and one of Julie's best friends, had helped them recruit his friend Leo as the Treasurer.

An incoming call notification popped up on the right-hand side of the computer screen, the name pushing a knife into Julie's heart.

Her father had reached out several times in the last few months, but outside the very brief texts with the barest of information, Julie hadn't responded. She didn't know how to. Not when every insight into her life widened the rift with her mother and reinforced her father's position in between them.

She watched the notification disappear, steeling herself for the inevitable voicemail. His gentle voice would be *just checking in, hope things are well, would love to hear from you. Call when you get the chance.* But Julie was still haunted by her mother admitting last year she partially blamed Julie for the death of Hannah.

After that, Julie had left without looking back.

"Jules, have you finished that fundraising plan?" Rachel's voice cut through the replay of Julie's last conversation with her mom.

Looking up, Julie met Rachel's golden brown eyes. "No, not yet. I can have it for you by the end of the week."

"That'd be great, thanks." Rachel was all business as she replaced her earbud and turned back to her laptop. Julie watched the thin gold bracelets tinkle against one another as her elegant friend typed. Glancing around the office, she avoided Ella's empty desk. As the resident on-tour publicist for Maven Media's music clients, her sister-from-another-mister was on tour with her fiancée's band. And with Julie's love, Anthony.

Her heart hurt at the thought. He was due home any day, but it wasn't soon enough.

She side-eyed Ruby, anxious to find what Anthony had seen in her. Julie always tried to come up empty-handed, and was subsequently reminded of being in India and addressing her old habits that had contributed to her being so miserable.

Comparing herself to others was one of them.

Taking a deep breath, Julie tried to release the thought. Ruby was sweet and funny, supportive and good at her job. She had a nice smile, pretty hair, thin legs that looked good in everything. Of course guys — Anthony — liked her. Just like how they liked Julie's banter and wit, her thick thighs and golden hair. They were different, and sometimes they were the same.

She just wished she didn't have to work with the woman.

Ruby glanced up, catching Julie's eyes. She felt the heat rise in her cheeks and looked away, pretending to busy herself with her computer.

Slick.

Julie sighed, groaning when another incoming call popped up on her computer. But the anxiety in her chest quickly disappeared with the name of the caller.

"Hey, Anthony."

"Hey there, sunshine." Julie's body flushed at the sound of his voice, silk on skin. "So I may have gotten back to New York City without knowing where the lady resides. I was hoping to surprise her, but I'm not that smooth. Any chance you could help a man hopelessly in love?"

The need to smile and cry all at once hurt her cheeks, and Julie covered her face with her hands.

He was finally home.

4

Anthony paced outside of Julie's apartment building, debating whether to buzz her neighbor to let him in or to greet his beloved on the street.

Fuck it.

He buzzed the neighbor. Julie promised she'd text them so they knew to let Anthony in, and when the buzz answered his prayers he was up the stairs three at a time. Having gotten back that morning, he'd taken a quick shower at the apartment he lived in with his dad before taking off.

He needed her.

The neighbor — a short, rotund man with a mop of white hair — stood on the landing.

"Ay, you must be the ineffable Anthony Russo."

The man cracked a lopsided smile and shuffled closer to Anthony.

"I'm whoever Ms. Milligan needs, sir." He smiled and held out his hand. "And you are?"

"Just call me Carl. If you're a friend of Juliette's, you're a friend of mine." Despite thin skin pressed into wrinkles like the rings of a tree, Carl's handshake was firm. Strong. Carl's steely eyes stared into Anthony's. He'd used Julie's given name, a fact she shared with virtually no one.

Anthony was nervous about Julie living alone in New York City, especially when he was away. But after meeting Carl, he knew without a doubt that this man would protect Julie as his own.

"Likewise, Carl." The key was clasped between their two palms. Anthony peeled it with his hand as he released the shake. "Thanks again, and please let me know if you ever need anything."

Carl tipped his head and turned back to his own door, shuffling in and closing it with a soft click.

Anthony frantically turned his key in the lock, pushing the heavy door open and being hit with the only smell he wanted to breathe until his dying day. Leaning against the closed door, he closed his eyes. Rose and vanilla, warmth and golden light filled his senses. He'd been away from the sun for so long, but now here he was. So close he could almost taste it.

He breathed, wanting to fill his bones with the love he'd been away from. When he finally opened his eyes, he was greeted with a spacious living room and a small kitchen. He'd been given the virtual tour when Julie first moved in, and again with each new addition or design change to the space, but the glitchy screen and bad lighting could never do the apartment justice.

She'd outfitted the space with a beautiful cream and fuchsia rug, the swirled design ending in diamonds and mandalas. The black sofa and matching love seat were chic against a wallpapered wall, the gold damask on a dark background adding an air of modern nobility to the room. A large TV stood atop a well-filled bookcase, and shelves lined the walls with a variety of trinkets and plants. A photo of a young Julie with an older man and another picture of a young Julie and an even younger girl were the only two photographs in the space.

They were reminiscent of the photos he'd found earlier that year in his father's closet. Grainy, blurred family photos hiding the one portrait of Gideon's mom, letters scrawled in her cursive, evidence of an affair between a married man and the widowed wife of that man's brother. Anthony ran his hand through his still-damp hair, fingering the scar hidden beneath the locks. He'd have to tell Julie at some point. Especially since her best friend Ella would also be made aware of the secret, thanks to Gideon.

He sighed and walked through the small kitchen, wanting to forget the real world for a few hours while he basked in the light of the woman he loved and hadn't held in his arms in months. Anthony stopped at the open door of a bedroom. Everything screamed Julie, from the two-door closet to the stack of design magazines beside a small TV on top of a modern dresser. Delicate watercolor nudes in blues and reds and blacks adorned the wall in black frames, plants lined the window sills. One wall was a sherbet orange, pulling the oranges from the bedspread and pillows reminiscent of India.

Anthony turned back to the living room and bit his lip, looking around. In his haste to see her, he'd forgotten flowers, ginger beer, anything to add to his return. He'd have to buzz Carl again if he left, and he didn't want to bother the old man again.

He didn't have to think too long on the matter;

the sound of heels on the landing outside the apartment made his heart race, the fumbling key in the lock sending it into overdrive.

5

Julie didn't remember throwing her bag on the couch, only the run-and-jump that led to her legs wrapped around Anthony's hips. Burying her face in his neck, she inhaled his warm ginger musk and tried to hold back her tears.

His chest was hard against hers, the corded muscles of his shoulders tense beneath her hands. His hands gripped her ass, pulling her even closer against him. The stiff ridge of him pressed against her core and begged for release.

"Oh, fuck, I missed you," he breathed into her hair.

"I missed you, Anthony."

She clung to him as she would a life raft in a storm, the turbulent waters of the last few months threatening to drown her. The weight of it eased itself from her shoulders as she collapsed into him.

"Tired?" His voice was low as he carried her to the bedroom. The quilted comforter was soft beneath her skin as he lowered her, the down comforter beneath that a cloud that caught her.

"Peaceful."

Julie stared up at the man before her. The swelling of her heart, the need to drop to her knees as she dropped his pants to worship him. His cerulean eyes stared into hers as he ran a hand through his mop of black hair. He was scruffy, his clothes draping across his body in ways they hadn't before. The dark circles beneath his eyes were in stark contrast to the rose of his cheeks. She watched his arms flex as he reached for her, fingers trailing the length of buttons on her shirt before landing at the waist of her pencil skirt. The tips found their way beneath the band and pulled. A wicked smile crossed his face.

"Peaceful? Would you like me to bring you to heaven?"

"I'm already there." She smiled and raised her eyebrows before they burst out laughing.

"Oh, the cheese! How I've missed you." Anthony's laugh grew louder as he knelt over her, his lips grazing her neck. Julie's laughter turned to a gasp. A moan soon followed as his tongue traced the line of her ear, his teeth nibbling on the lobe. Julie pushed against him, her fingers threading through his hair. When his mouth reached her neck, she gasped, clutching him tighter to her. His large hands spanned her hips, roaming across her body.

Anthony pulled back just enough to stare into her eyes. "I want to worship you." He sealed his words with a kiss, one full of longing, before kneeling on the ground between her legs.

The ache between her thighs sent waves of desire rushing through her body. Julie sat up on her elbows, needing to watch him. She'd been away from him so long, there was a part of her that was worried he was a fantasy, a ghost, and would disappear just as quickly as he'd arrived.

He wound soft kisses up one leg, starting at her ankle. Lingering behind her knee, one hand reached up her skirt and gripped her thigh. His fingers toyed with the crotch of her lacy underwear as he moved his lips to the other leg. Julie watched him in a haze as he made his way up, goosebumps erupting across her skin as he gave the other side the same respect as the last. He looked up and held her gaze, both hands slowly pulling the underwear down her thighs and over where he'd lain his kisses.

"You're so beautiful," Anthony murmured, trailing kisses along her thighs, peeling her skirt up to her hips as he went.

With each touch, her body cried out for more. His lips were electric, his hands along her skin burning. She couldn't remember the last time she'd felt so alive.

Until his tongue dragged through her folds. Julie fell back on the bed, her body shaking from the sensation. The heat of his mouth added to the inferno raging in her body. Anthony took his time flicking his tongue over her clit before pulling it into his mouth and sucking. He buried his face in her heat, licking and sucking until she thought she'd explode from the pleasure. He pushed a finger into her wet center, adding a second, a third, gradually pulling them out before pushing them back in, his finger tips pressing against her sensitive inner wall. Julie cried out, hands twisting the bedsheets. His tongue working her bundle of nerves while his fingers pumped faster. Her muscles tightened, the edge calling her name.

He slowed and leaned in, his mouth pressing against her with an intense focus. Euphoria rippled through her body as the world around her spun. When Julie opened her eyes, Anthony was still between her legs, slowly lapping at her center. She sighed. A muffled laugh against her crotch tickled before turning into desperate need. Anthony worked his way in kisses up her body before settling above her, over her, his thick biceps carrying his weight as he gazed into her eyes.

6

Anthony looked down at Julie, his love, his life, his everything. Her rosy cheeks and glassy eyes, the tangle of blond locks spread over the bed, wet lips calling to him. Being away from her for so long had been difficult, but the reward of being in her arms almost made it worth it.

Julie ran her hands through his hair and over his face, and he turned to kiss her fingers as they trailed over his skin. He kissed his way up her arms, ending at her full lips. He needed to drink her, all of her. The kiss was sloppy, slick, both of them thirsty and desperate for more. It grew more fervent as he pushed her up the bed, wrapping her legs around his hips.

"I need you," she rasped between frantic kisses.

She whimpered into him, hands grasping for his hard cock, thick and throbbing as her fingers stroked his length.

"I've always needed you." Anthony kissed her, leaving a trail to her breasts. He teased her nipples with his tongue, relishing the way her body squirmed under his.

But he needed more. He grunted, fingers desperately finding her sopping core and positioning his tip at her center. He watched her face as he eased into her warmth. Her body arched as he slowly pushed, every gasp, every whimper music to his ears as she opened to him. He pushed her legs wider, needing his hips to meet hers. Needing to reclaim her.

Anthony kissed her golden skin, teeth nipping and pulling at her ear as he pulled out. Julie's fingers dug into his shoulders, her breath hot in his ear. He thrust into her, hard, relishing the way she moaned his name and pushed herself against him. Her body trembled as he found rhythm. Every cell in his body was awake to her desire, her skin sliding against his, the clench of her hands against his arms and back, her heels digging into his ass.

The pressure building inside him was begging for release.

His thrusts became more insistent, his cock hard as stone as he thumbed the sensitive bundle at her apex. He growled as her muscles contracted around him, her gasps reaching a fever pitch. Anthony shuddered against her, his own climax meeting hers in a fierce wave of ecstasy. He fell onto her, breathless, his heartbeat matching hers. He breathed in the warm scent of rose and vanilla, the heady scent of sex and sweat. Julie's fingers danced on his skin as their breathing steadied.

Anthony settled his chin on her flushed chest, rolling off her just enough to ease the pressure of his muscled frame. Her smile was sleepy, but her eyes were still dark with desire.

He smirked. She was insatiable.

"What's that look, hot shot?"

Her voice was low, husky, dripping with need. He playfully nipped at her nipple before diving his mouth onto hers. Julie met his languid kisses, rolling them onto their sides. Anthony wrapped one arm under her neck while the other stroked her hair.

She was the only thing in his life that made sense.

This was what life was about, and goddamnit if he wasn't going to do everything in his power to make her officially his.

7

The smooth skin beneath Julie's cheek was heaven, a cloud that caught her as she fell into bliss last night. She pressed against the warmth, entwining her legs with the muscled ones beside her. Anthony's arm pulled her tighter against him as he pressed a soft kiss to her forehead. She felt the smile as he did so, felt the way his heartbeat matched her own.

This wasn't a dream.

"Good morning, my love." His voice was gravelly from neglect.

They hadn't done much talking last night.

Julie smiled at the thought, stretching her stiff limbs. "Good morning, sweetness." She lingered her lips on the space above his heart.

"Don't you have work?" he murmured into the top of her head.

"It'll be fine, I'm sure Ella's not going in today either. Rachel knows you guys came home."

He chuckled. "If you say so. I guess that means breakfast's in order?"

"Psh, breakfast is always in order. But first, coffee." Julie smiled against his skin, willing herself to break the contact by sitting up. Now that Anthony was here, her apartment finally felt like home. When he padded into the kitchen with her and got the coffee brewing, that feeling was reaffirmed. Well over six feet, it was more than the space he filled. He moved with a feline grace, his energy relaxed and open as if he belonged there, had fallen asleep every night in that bed and woken every morning to make her coffee. As if being surrounded by her made him as much at home as he did for her.

"Mugs?" He turned to look at her, eyes cobalt in the morning light. Anthony leaned one arm against the soapstone counter, thighs stretching the fabric of his briefs. His thick cock twitched beneath the cloth, a salacious smile reaching his lips.

"I always thought you wanted coffee first in the morning, but I will happily oblige."

Julie smiled, reaching in a top cabinet for two

mugs. Her face had betrayed the heat coursing through her body. They had plenty of time to play, but she really did need her coffee first.

Anthony poured and they sat on the couch in silence. Julie watched his thin lips purse to blow on the hot liquid, wincing as he took a sip, arms flexing as he set the mug on the glass coffee table. She could watch him forever.

"What are you thinkin', sunshine?"

Her eyes rose to meet his, a smile flirting at the corners of his lips.

"Just about you." Julie blew on her coffee before taking a scalding sip.

"I never stop thinking about you," he said, rubbing her calf with calloused hands while looking around the room. "Have you finished outfitting your office and the guest bedroom?"

Julie had to stop herself from spitting the coffee back into her mug at the thought of the kids room. "Done with the office but not the bedroom." She couldn't shake the heaviness of the white lie. "How was tour? I know you gave me the short version last night." Anything to change the topic.

"It was good. Great." Anthony sighed. "Honestly, it was a dream. Imagine Dragons especially, they loved our sound and energy. But I'm so fucking tired. And... things were a little tense with Gideon."

"Why?" Julie sat up, her guilt turning to anxiety at the mention of her best friend's fiancé. Gideon had broken Ella's heart once before, when he'd tried to go sober the first time. Being on tour as the front man for a hot indie rock band was a lifestyle that didn't lend itself well to staying clean.

"So before we left for tour, I found a box in my dad's closet. We'd had a fight and he'd left, and... I had a moment of weakness. I went looking for a couple bottles of alcohol my dad had brought to a band meeting."

Julie went still, her eyes burning into his. Trying to steady her breathing, she wanted nothing more than to question him. To ask if he'd found relief in amber liquid and forgotten nights. But pushing him would cause him to retreat, or at the very least add a tension to this conversation she didn't want to have.

He took a deep breath. "While I was looking, I ended up going through his closet. I just had to know if he would actually leave alcohol alone with me. I needed to know if he was trying to tempt me. I found the whiskey and — I swear to god, Julie — I dumped it down the drain. But I also found an old box. It held an old bible, a leather necklace cord, an envelope, and a stack of letters."

Anthony put his head in his hands, a shaky breath coursing through his hunched shoulders. She rested a hand on his back, unable to decipher where this story was going. The assortment of items was puzzling.

"The envelope had a bunch of old pictures. Family pictures. Me, my mom, Gideon. Gideon's dad. But it also had a portrait of Gideon's mom, Amelia. And the letters... They were from her. Amelia. To my dad."

Julie's breath hitched, the realization hitting her.

"I stupidly told Gideon before we left for tour. He wanted to discuss it with them, and I wanted to wait until after. He eventually agreed, but it was tense whenever it was just the two of us. And now we're back from tour."

Anthony leaned against the couch, his gaze glued to a space on the carpet. Julie bit her lower lip. At least the conversation hadn't gone where she'd feared. Anytime he brought up Gideon or alcohol she tensed. Gideon had fallen off the wagon and while she wanted to believe both he and Anthony had reached a place of not wanting to backslide, Julie knew addiction didn't care about shit like that.

"When do you think you guys will talk to your parents?"

"No idea." Anthony shrugged. "My dad said he wants to go to our house in Sugar Grove for a few weeks, so probably once he comes back. Gideon might talk to his mom before that, though." Standing, he reached out a hand to pull Julie up from the couch. "I don't want to think anymore about that. I just want to go back to bed."

Julie laughed as she gripped his hand. "And what do you want to do once you're in bed?"

"Do I really have to tell you?" He backed into her room, pulling her along. "You know all I want to do is sleep."

"Ooo, yeah. Just sleep." Julie waggled her eyebrows at the gorgeous hunk of a man leading her to bed, pushing down the guilt of being dishonest with him when he'd been vulnerable.

A conversation for another time.

8

"I can't believe Tom just up and left," Gideon said through a mouthful of Spicy Sweet Chili Doritos.

"Right? I thought after tour he'd want to chill here," Anthony said.

Guess he didn't want to spend more time with me.

Anthony took a seat across from Gideon. He was trying not to treat the apartment as his, instead spending most of his time at Julie's. But the longer Tom was gone, the more Anthony enjoyed the stillness. The reprieve from his dad stalking away from him. Always away.

He cradled his water glass, watching his cousin plow the bag in his lap. Gideon had lost some of the weight he'd put on during tour — Anthony had lost some on tour and was starting to gain it back — and had a look of contentment permanently fixed to his face. Anthony knew in large part it was because of Ella. His cousin had trimmed his hair, and his blue eyes surveyed the room.

"Have you seen your mom?" Anthony blurted.

Gideon settled his gaze on Anthony, slowly chewing what was in his mouth and setting the bag aside. "No, not yet."

Anthony nodded. "You know we need to talk about how to... you know."

"Yeah. I know."

Ice filled the air. Gideon eventually shifted his gaze and sighed. He always bowed to Anthony. It'd been like that since they were kids.

"I think we should talk to them alone, separately. I'll talk to my mom, you talk to your dad. And then..." Gideon shrugged.

"And then we'll reconvene and see how to move forward?" Anthony asked. "Maybe we should ask them together?"

"What would be the point in that? Besides everyone talking over one another. And they can corroborate any story they want at that point. If we get them alone, what they say might not line up."

"But they might be more likely to tell us the truth, if both of us are asking. And if we ask separately, we might get the timing off and one could warn the other."

Gideon sighed. "Fine. You win. We should wait until Tom is back for good."

"I could just tell him we need to talk and ask when he'll be back." A loose thread on his jeans begged for attention. He needed to talk to his dad about more than just the affair. It'd make for several conversations over several days. Uncharted territory for them.

"Okay, that sounds good. Let me know what he says." Gideon picked up his bag of chips, resuming the crunching and finger-licking. "How are things with Julie?"

Anthony tried to hide the smile, his gold goddess haunting his every waking moment. "Great. Been staying a lot at her place." He loved picturing her in her own space, holding her coffee and laughing with him. Watching her skin kissed by sunlight, eyes blue diamond brilliant as they shared her most intimate feelings. They'd fallen in love with one another in every moment they spent together since Anthony had come back. Gideon's snicker brought him back to the dark living room of the apartment he shared with his pissed-off but absent father.

"What?"

"I just know that look. When do you think you'll move in together?"

It was Anthony's turn to bark out a laugh. "I don't think anytime soon. She's enjoying being alone in her apartment, and she is very against sharing her spare bedroom with my instruments."

One night, her back against his chest as they snuggled on the couch with a movie, he'd jokingly mentioned keeping a guitar or keyboard in the spare bedroom. She'd stiffened in his arms for the briefest of moments before chuckling, her voice soft with an, "I don't think so."

"What is it, Ant?"

Anthony looked at his cousin. "I dunno, I vaguely mentioned leaving an instrument and she got kind of... stiff. Off? I don't know. I didn't want to push so we had a good laugh and that was that."

"Does she not have room for a guitar?"

"I don't know, I haven't seen the spare bedroom."

"At all?"

"At all."

Gideon's brow furrowed. "That's a little odd. Right? I think that's a bit weird."

Anthony shrugged, reaching for the bag of chips. Was it weird? He hadn't given it too much thought. He had been to her place many times in the past couple of weeks. The office across from the bathroom almost always had the door open to allow light into the space, and from what he could gather was fairly packed with shelving, paperwork, and an assortment of craft supplies. But the spare bedroom door had always been closed when he ventured down the hall to the bathroom. This was the woman he wanted to spend the rest of his life with. She'd held the death of her younger sister close to her chest, not even telling Ella until push came to shove. When she'd finally let Anthony in, it had been after he'd torn down his own walls. After showing her he wasn't going anywhere.

After she'd come home from India, he thought they'd sealed their fate without any walls. And maybe they had, but now he couldn't help but feel the walls had been replaced with a single closed door.

9

The navy bedspread beneath Julie was soft, cotton and down. Matching pillows propped her up. The audience of stuffed animals sat beside her, watching. Her phone, heavy with the weight of knowing she needed to call her father, stared up at her. It'd be so much easier if Carty would just call again, and she could just answer. Pretend nothing had changed.

She took a deep breath.

"Juliette?" His soft voice was tinged with disbelief. Julie scrunched her face at being that shit of a daughter.

"Hey, Dad." She chewed her lower lip. How did sorry even begin to cover the way she'd blown him off, left him holding the bag between her absence, her sister's death, and her mother's blame?

"It's so nice to hear from you. I missed your voice, honey. Are you okay?" The creak of his favorite armchair in the family room brought a flood of memories. Julie closed her eyes to relive them. The kindness in his eyes, the sadness in the slope of his shoulders.

"Yeah, Dad. Things are great. The apartment's nice and work's good." She took a deep breath, steeling herself for the amount of information she was divulging. "I'm seeing someone and it's pretty serious."

"Oh. Oh, wow." Carty had never had to deal with his little girl dating. In her parents' eyes, Julie had focused on school. Behind closed doors, she'd focused on one-night stands and flings. She'd never so much as mentioned a partner in front of them.

"Do I need to give him some sort of talk to make sure he's treating you right? I mean, if he needs a talk for that, he doesn't deserve you."

Julie smiled. "Thanks, but it's okay. He's wonderful."

"Do I get any more information on this fella?" Carty chuckled, chair creaking.

His words sobered Julie, the real reason for her call rising to the surface.

"How's Mom?"

A heavy sigh escaped through the phone. "The same, Juliette. The same. Her perky, fiery self until something reminds her of you. Or Hannah. Then she retreats until suddenly she's back, and we start all over."

"Does she still blame me?"

"I don't know, honey."

The exasperation in his voice twisted the knife in Julie's heart. His life had been filled with pain. Her mom blamed Julie for most of it.

"Juliette, you know she will never come to you first."

Julie chewed her lower lip. Pride was the trunk of their family tree; it coursed through Julie's veins as much as it did her mother's. But Julie had the softness from her father as her roots, recognizing when to push that wall of pride aside. Sometimes.

"She should come to me first, though, Dad."

"I don't dispute that, but you know she won't. In all my days, I've never seen that woman back down. I think in all the time I've been with her, she's apologized once."

"Yeah, that sounds like Mom." Julie rolled her eyes. "Would she even pick up if I called?"

She waited through the creaks and the sighs, picturing his rough hand running over a bald head in a habit from hairier days. Julie smiled at the thought. She missed her father, missed him even more for all the pain she'd helped cause. He didn't deserve to be the wall between two prideful women.

"You know what, Dad? I'll come home. You shouldn't have to keep being the go-between. Can you please tell her I'm planning on coming home to speak to her, so she can be prepared? I don't want her to feel ambushed."

"Really?" Carty's voice lifted in hope.

"Really. I'll let you know when once I figure out my work schedule."

They signed off and Julie looked around the room. It was waiting for an infusion of color, of life. Of laughter that belonged to someone truly loved. If she was ever going to be the woman — the mother — she wanted to be, Julie needed to forgive her own.

10

"Hey, sunshine," Anthony said. The only sun he needed filled the doorframe, her smile lighting her face and his heart. Every second away was a second too long.

Julie shook her head, moving aside so he could step into the small entryway. He grabbed her arm before she could fully turn away, planting a kiss on those velvety lips. She opened to him and laced her arms around his neck. Anthony delved his tongue into her mouth, needing to explore every crevice he'd missed over the last few days they'd been part. Frantic, needy, desperate. She moaned into him, her hips pressing against his hardening member, fingers tracing the skin above his waistband. His hands found the smooth path to her breasts and squeezed.

The peak of her nipples pressed through the lacy bra and Anthony's cock responded.

"Oh, pardon me."

Anthony pulled back, setting himself between Julie and the building's hallway. Carl stood in front of his door, shielding his eyes from where they stood. The heat rose in Anthony's cheeks.

"Oh, um, sorry, Carl. We'll head inside."

"Oh, SHIT! I'm sorry, Carl!" Julie covered her mouth, a bright red overtaking her fair skin.

The elderly man chuckled. "Eh, we've all been there. Just going to get the mail. Y'all doing alright?"

"Yep, all good. You?" Anthony threw him a small smile, one hand ready to push the door closed.

"Can't complain. I'll leave you to it." Carl tipped his head and turned toward the ancient olive green elevator. Anthony shut the door before there was another chance to make eye contact. Leaning against the heavy door, he bowed with laughter. Julie's own echoed through the apartment, in between gasps for air.

"Oh, man. I'll never be able to look at him again. Hell, he'll never be able to look at me again either." She wiped tears from her eyes, heading into the kitchen.

Anthony's face hurt from laughing so hard. He

followed, sitting on the couch while he watched her reach into the fridge for ginger beer. Julie's shirt rode up, revealing the barest hint of skin on her lower back. The slice of heaven disappeared when she rose, replaced with her outstretched arm, a glass bottle in hand, reaching towards him. Julie took a seat beside him and crossed her legs over his. They clinked bottles and drank the spicy nonalcoholic brew.

"So, hot stuff. Stud muffin. How's it going?"

He chuckled. "Better now. How about you, sweet thang?"

Julie's excitement was palpable as she launched into the nonprofit she was building at Maven Media. Permits and members and fundraising plans filled the small apartment and Anthony could only smile and listen. Office life was a far cry from his own, and the way Julie found enjoyment in it made him want to listen for hours. Anything that made her happy, made him happy.

Anthony smiled when she finally took a breath and relaxed her arms from their waving emphasis. Lifting the bottle to her lips, Julie frowned when she realized it was empty. Anthony laughed.

"Damn, I hadn't even realized I finished it." Her pout was somehow just as lovely as her smile. It made her look innocent, naive. It was easy for him to see her as a child, and the sweetness nearly melted him.

He stood and took her empty glass alongside his. "Same. How about you order whatever food you want for lunch and I'll pay?"

Julie chewed her lower lip before a small smile started to spread. "Well, alright. If you insist. Want anything in particular?"

"Nope, whatever the lady wishes." Anthony set the bottles in the sink, planting a soft kiss on Julie's forehead as he made his way to the bathroom. The office door across from his destination was closed, but the door to the spare bedroom at the end of the long hallway allowed a sliver of light into the narrow space. Anthony nearly stopped in his tracks at the sight.

He'd never seen that door open.

Anthony couldn't believe it. Julie had evaded the room in conversation, sticking strictly to it being a spare bedroom but getting stiff anytime he mentioned wanting to see it. But he could read her like an open book, and the slight fluster she took on paired with the quick topic change always made him feel like she was hiding something.

Anthony tried glancing into the room before

entering the bathroom and again after leaving the restroom. Neither glimpse gave him any info aside from white walls and what looked like the footboard to a bed. He could hear Julie's muffled voice in the kitchen ordering their food. He took a deep breath.

His finger brushed the door, nudging it open an extra inch.

Definitely a bed. Navy bedspread with matching pillows. Stuffed animals?

He pushed the door another inch.

Nightstand and the corner of... a guitar?

"Ant?"

Anthony started down the hall as she came into view at the other end.

"Everything okay?" She peered behind him before returning her attention to him. Her smile was nervous as he dropped another kiss on her forehead, the patter of her bare feet following him into the kitchen.

"Peachy keen." Anthony hoped he'd been able to keep the confusion from his tone. But the fear in Julie's eyes made him think he wasn't as good at hiding things as he thought. He cleared his throat. "What'd you decide to order?"

"Mexican." She shuffled towards him, wrapping

her arms around his waist and gazing up at him, eyes searching his face. "You sure everything's okay?"

He smiled, reassurance mixed with the lie. "Positive. Just a bit tired and very much looking forward to snuggling on that couch with you."

11

Julie sucked in a breath, not listening to the conversation between Rachel and Ella as they dissolved into a fit of laughter. Girl's Night was a long time coming, but having all three of their schedules work out at the same time was nearly impossible.

Miraculously, they had managed to find a night, and here they sat in Rachel's apartment — where Rachel still lived with their mutual friend Ben and where Ella and Julie used to reside — with a smorgasbord of Chinese, a box of Cabernet wine as an homage to their college days, and a bottle of Espolon tequila to mix in their cans of cucumber mint seltzer. A favorite rom-com played on the large flat-screen TV before them, but Julie knew they would switch to a B horror movie soon. After she got the guts to tell them what she'd done to Anthony.

"Jules, you alright?" Ella's cheeks were round with her smile, red with the flush of alcohol and laughter.

"Guys, I — I fucked up."

Ella stopped chowing down on the fried dumplings and Rachel's eyes widened as she refilled their wine glasses and began getting their tequila seltzer ready.

"So I never actually told Anthony about the fostering."

Julie cringed, her eyes closing to the look of horror written across her friends' faces. If she couldn't see them, they couldn't see her.

Right?

The weighted silence ultimately won out, and Julie cracked an eyelid. Ella and Rachel stared at her, mouths agape.

Julie took another deep breath. "I just... I don't know, I didn't know how to tell him. We had just gotten to a good place, and then he was on tour. And I missed him so much while he was gone. So I've just been wanting to enjoy my time with him, you know?"

Rachel held Julie's gaze. "Have you guys discussed the future at all? And it's not like he's flat-out asked you if you've applied to be a foster parent, right?"

"Nothing past 'I love you, I want to be with you,'" Julie said, chewing her lower lip. "But he's been wanting to see the apartment, and you know I turned one of the extra rooms into a bedroom. He thinks it's just a spare bedroom for guests, but I saw him peek inside because I stupidly left the door ajar. There are stuffed animals and a beginner guitar and other knickknacks for kids. He seemed a bit put-off, but I don't know what he saw."

Tequila and seltzer never tasted so good.

"Oh, Jules. You have to tell him." Ella stared at her best friend, dumpling in hand.

"I know, I know. But what if that's what pushes him away?"

"Then he wasn't right for you anyway." Rachel shrugged. "But this is huge, and it could end your relationship. He's going to find out one way or another, so you might as well do it soon. You don't want a kid to show up and then have Anthony show up and leave — that would destroy the kid."

Julie cradled her seltzer. She hadn't even thought

about the emotional toll that could have on the child, if events played out like that.

And that's a negative parenting point, Julie.

"Maybe I'll wait until after he and Gideon have settled the whole affair thing. I know he's really preoccupied with that."

"Wait, what?" Rachel stared at Julie. "Girl, you are dropping so many bombs. What affair?"

Ella piped in. "Apparently Anthony found evidence of an affair between his dad and Gideon's mom. It was after Gideon's dad passed but before Anthony's mom left."

"Jeeesus. You guys sure do have a lot of drama. But still, you need to tell him ASAP. It's not really fair for either of you to invest in a relationship when you're withholding a potential dealbreaker." Rachel downed most of her wine.

Julie turned back to the TV, watching the love interests reunite on the Manhattan Bridge as the camera pulled out and the credits started to roll. Rachel was always the practical one in the group. No holds barred honest, ambitious, unapologetic. Julie knew she was right. But the reality of having a child and needing to consider how every single one of her decisions had consequences was something that had really only been a theory, but was now being put into practice, like a ton of bricks. What if she was a bad parent? What if she was unprepared? What if she told Anthony what she'd done and he backed out? What if she ended up not fostering?

What if her holding back the information pushed Anthony away?

12

Gideon sat at the island across from Anthony, who had hot sauce slathered on his hands and across his face. Enjoying his own pizza in peace was impossible for Anthony while his cousin made such a mess with chicken wings. His stomach turned in nausea and he set his half-eaten slice down.

"Dude, could you chill?"

"What do you mean?"

"You need a bib and some baby wipes." Anthony shook his head and looked away. "You and Ella really were made for each other."

Gideon's eyes turned steely. "Talk shit about me all you want but leave Ella out of this. Besides, it's not like Julie's some prissy eater. I've seen her go ham on some ribs before."

They both chuckled, easing the tension. Slightly.

Anthony picked up his pizza. "So, my dad's coming back in a couple of days. I figure the day after, I could make dinner and you and your mom can show up?"

"That won't be suspicious?"

"In what way?"

"When have you ever made dinner for your dad?" Gideon chuckled.

"I have." Anthony shrugged. "I could also just tell him we need to talk and that I'll make dinner."

"I honestly don't know how I'll get my mom out, though. If I say your dad invited us, she'll probably text him."

Anthony brushed the pizza flour from his hands, his mouth working the last piece of crust while he thought.

"Could you just tell her you want to take her to dinner and show up at the apartment? I don't think she'd ever been here before."

"And then when she sees it's an apartment building, have her back out?" Gideon barked out a laugh. "Yeah, that'll go over real well."

"I don't know, man. When you get here just tell her I made dinner and we're expecting you guys. Knowing your mom, she'll feel bad leaving me hanging and will come up, even if she knows something's up." Anthony sighed, wishing he had another slice to occupy his hands with. But they'd plowed through the pizza and Gideon was working his way through the hot wings.

Talking about Amelia, talking about the affair, made him ache over his own mom. Christine had disappeared when he was eighteen. Last year his dad had let slip she'd also had trouble with alcohol. Anthony had scoured the internet trying to find her and, when he did, had found the courage to send her a message. Months later, Christine Scott had met Anthony at a fancy restaurant here in New York City. Minutes later, she'd told him everything he'd known in his heart and feared. So he walked out. Blocked her on Facebook and ignored her calls.

This time, he'd been the one to walk out on her.

Having that conversation and making that move had given him a sense of power he'd longed for, and it helped ease the pain of not knowing why his own mom would disappear and ignore him. But it hadn't erased it. Anthony was coming to terms with the idea it would never fully go away.

Gideon slurped his fingers, pulling Anthony back to the apartment. "Do you think your dad will keep alcohol in the apartment going forward?"

The question nearly knocked the wind out of Anthony.

"God, I hope not." He narrowed his eyes at his cousin. "Why?"

"Just curious. Still a bit shocked he even did it in the first place, but if he hadn't, you wouldn't have found the box of shit. And we wouldn't be in this position." Gideon stood and stretched as he made his way into the kitchen to wash his hands.

Anthony chewed his lower lip. He was pissed, disappointed at his father for bringing alcohol to a band meeting in the apartment when three of the band members were sober. When he'd found the bottle of whiskey in his dad's closet, he'd replaced his relief with anger. The sharp honey of the liquid burned his nostrils when he'd poured it down the drain, called to the space between his bones to let it in.

Let it in, just one more time.

He hadn't even really missed it before that night. He hadn't missed it since. But there was something about having it in his space, in his home, that had turned it into something different.

Anthony watched Gideon meander back into the living room, grabbing the TV remote as he plopped down. Anthony had never really had trouble with missing alcohol, but Gideon had. And his curiosity of the potential for more hidden alcohol sent a wave of fear through Anthony. His cousin has slipped up once before.

Would he again?

13

The brisk air followed Julie back into the office building. It smelled cold, like stone or ice, winter on the wings of the wind bursting off the East River, flowing in the tunnels made by the tall buildings and narrow streets.

Julie began removing her scarf as she entered the elevator in an attempt to ignore the bright red hair glowing beneath the gold light. But the tension couldn't be avoided, nor Ruby's stern greeting.

"Hey." It was all Julie could muster in response to the woman that had slept with Anthony, the woman who worked across the way from her, whose laugh echoed throughout the office, every day.

From her periphery, Julie saw Ruby take a deep breath and turn to face her.

"Julie, I think we should talk."

"Oh? Why is that?" Julie couldn't keep the chill from her voice. Talking to Ruby Delacey was the last thing she wanted to do, but she couldn't figure out if it was more anxiety or hurt that kept her from extending a hand across the aisle.

"Seriously, Julie? You know why."

The elevator dinged open, both women glued to their spots. Julie tried to not roll her eyes as she turned to face Ruby. The door closed and the elevator shifted back to the ground floor.

Julie met Ruby's gaze. "Yeah, you're right. I do know why. I'm just not ready to."

"Well, when will you be ready?" Ruby shifted her weight.

"I don't know, and it shouldn't matter. We work in the same office but not in the same department." Julie pressed the elevator button for the floor they'd just left. "I'm cool if you're cool."

Hiding how very not true that was was nearly impossible, and the sigh from Ruby indicated she knew as much.

"It matters to me. Please let me know when you're ready."

As soon as the words left her lips, the elevator door opened and Ruby's heels clicked their way out.

Julie followed, taking her time as the curls of fire bounced against her adversary's straight back. She waited a moment before entering the office and was greeted with Ella and Priya's laughter. In the back, to the left of Julie's desk, Ruby stood beside Rachel's desk. Both women looked serious and spoke in hushed tones. Julie tried to hear what they were discussing as she made her way back but was only able to catch their parting words.

"Thanks, Rach." Ruby gave a small smile and caught Julie's eye before turning away.

Julie couldn't stop the pit from forming in her stomach, but tried sitting down as nonchalantly as possible. "What was that about?" She glanced at her friend, gauging if Rachel's stoic face would let anything up.

"Nothing." Rachel popped her headphones back in.

It wasn't an unusual response from her friend, her boss, but coming off the heels of Julie's terse conversation with Ruby and Ruby's hopeful, 'Thanks, Rach,' it was enough to make Julie worry that maybe she'd crossed a line.

14

Anthony looked around the apartment, the odor of melted cheese and red chili powder making his stomach turn.

He was not ready for tonight.

If there was one dish he knew how to make for important conversations, it was chicken enchiladas. They were Julie's favorite, one he'd mastered in an attempt to win her heart last year. Now he was banking on them being a good luck charm for when Gideon and his mom arrived.

Anthony glanced at the clock. They'd be here soon, and his dad was in his room with the door closed. Anthony had texted him earlier in the week, asking him to come home, offering a home cooked meal. Leaving out the part about an ambush.

Tom had come home from their house in Sugar Grove a few days ago but Anthony had only seen him in passing. Interactions had been limited to grunts and the occasional, "How are things?" Anthony knew he'd gone behind his dad's back in speaking with his estranged mom, but he couldn't understand how or why his dad could be so cold to him for so long. Not like it would end anytime soon, what with tonight on the horizon. Anthony sighed and pulled out a serving spatula.

"Hey, dad?" he called down the hallway. "Dinner's ready."

He served himself as the door slowly creaked open and the heavy footsteps of a large, middle-aged man walked into the kitchen. Problems aside, Tom had come home a few pounds heavier and with a glow about him. He seemed happy, and more willing to interact with Anthony than before he'd left for the month.

"Smells good. Thanks." Tom grabbed a plate and started dishing, avoiding eye contact with Anthony.

The apartment intercom buzzed. Tom's gaze whipped up to meet Anthony's.

Looking away, Anthony went to the box and buzzed them up.

"Who is that?" Tom asked.

"Gideon, I invited him over for dinner."

Anthony unlocked the door, trying to still his shaking hands under his dad's scrutiny. But there was nothing he could do when Gideon and Amelia walked in. Tom nearly dropped his plate but dropped his jaw instead.

"A-Amelia." He regained his composure and moved to greet them.

Inside, Anthony made eye contact with Gideon as he grabbed two more plates and started dishing, letting his aunt and dad catch up. They laughed about something on their way to the dining table with their plates.

"Well, this is certainly a surprise. I haven't seen you in ages, Mel." Tom returned Amelia's sweet smile, but it fell once he remembered Anthony and Gideon. He sat back, resting his hands in his lap.

Anthony shifted in his seat and took a bite of the enchiladas. There was no easy way to do this.

Gideon cleared his throat. "We, um, we wanted to talk to you guys."

Amelia stopped chewing while Tom shook his head.

"We didn't know how to go about it but... we know about the affair." Anthony could hardly hear what he was saying. It felt like a dream, something happening to someone other than him. The distance between him and his father seemed to grow across the table, the heavy silence taking a seat between them.

The clink of Amelia setting her fork down broke the barriers, a sigh landing in her hand as she rested her head.

"Well, then. That's really a bummer, I'm sorry. How did you find out?"

Anthony chewed his lower lip, not sure of how much to divulge. Lately, it was rare for him to get this opportunity to speak candidly, honestly, with his father. He might as well make the most of it.

"My dad brought whiskey to a band meeting, a few weeks before tour. It set me on edge, and we were in the middle of an... I don't know, an argument? Because I'd reached out to my mom when he'd asked me not to." Amelia's eyes went wide at the mention of Christine, and Tom held his head in both hands. Anthony continued. "One of the nights he was gone, I went looking for the bottle. I just needed to know if he'd kept it in the house. He did. I dumped it down the sink, I swear on everyone's life, but I found an old box. It had a bunch of stuff — I think a bible, a necklace, some photos — and it also had letters. A bunch of letters, from you, Aunt Mel."

"We thought about talking to you guys before tour, but we didn't want to risk ruining the band dynamic for so long and during such a huge opportunity," Gideon said. "But guys, we have to talk about this."

Gideon's face was starting to fall, his skin taking on a shade of red Anthony was unused to, his eyes becoming glassy. Gideon was usually the one that was good about keeping a straight face. He was usually the one who kept everything under lock and key. Anthony had only ever seen him break two other times: the loss of his dad, and the loss of Ella the first time. Seeing it now, he hadn't realized just how much this affected his cousin. Anthony had always felt like he'd been alone in the hurt. After all, the affair had occurred right before his mom walked out of his life without looking back.

The affair had ruined his family.

What had it done to Gideon?

"Boys, there's nothing to talk about. It happened years ago, it's over, we've moved on."

"Are you for real?" It slipped out before Anthony could stop himself. The absurdity of the comment was almost too much, and he barked out a laugh.

Tom's eyes were steely as they bore into Anthony's. "Yeah, I'm fucking for real."

"Dad… you guys had an affair before Mom left. And the letters sound like it started right after Gideon's dad — your fucking brother — died. So yeah, we actually do have a lot to talk about."

Tom opened his mouth and Amelia reached out, placing a weathered hand on top of his. "Tom, honey, it's okay. We should talk about it." She turned to Gideon and Anthony. "I'm sorry, boys. Truly. It was a complicated time, and the way we handled it was… less than ideal. I'm more than happy to answer questions, but it might be better to discuss it separ—"

"Nah, we're going to talk about it right here, right now. Together. We do have questions, and I think we deserve all the answers." Anthony pushed his plate away and folded his arms. "Gideon, would you like to ask the first one?"

His cousin took a deep breath. "When did you guys start talking… romantically? Not necessarily when the affair actually started, but when it was obvious there was interest."

"Gideon, it was after we found out your father's illness was terminal." Amelia's voice cracked. "He — He was still alive when the interest was made known, but nothing was acted on until after. After he passed." She wiped her eyes and Gideon stared at his plate. "I'm so sorry, honey."

"Who made the first move?" Anthony clenched his jaw, realizing how badly he needed that question answered.

"We hugged and when we pulled back, we didn't let go," Tom said. "After that, we avoided being alone together, but there was one night... after he died, that was particularly bad. Mel was crying, and I hugged her. I held her. And then... we kissed."

Anthony stared at a spot in the center of the table, trying to find something interesting about it. The world around him pulsated, heaved, bled a fog that settled over him. The words flying around him dimmed and dropped until it was just him and that spot on the table, a spot filled with the image of his father falling in love with his brother's wife, forgetting his own at home. As much as Anthony knew his mom leaving was her own choice, hearing how his father pushed her away hurt almost as much.

He didn't try to fix their relationship.

He didn't do anything to keep their family together.

He actively worked against their family, taking what he wanted.

Anthony stood, his chair almost tipping backward. The conversation around him halted, tears falling from Gideon's cheeks, Amelia's head in her hands, Tom staring at the same spot Anthony had been staring at.

Anthony looked at his father. "Not only did you ruin our family, you did nothing to save it. No wonder mom left." He turned toward Amelia. "And you. You knew he was married. He was your husband's brother, of course that's going to cause some shit. For everyone. I don't know how to make this right, but I can't be here."

Gideon followed him into the hall, the door slamming behind them as they left their parents at the table.

15

"Are you okay?"

The man before Julie looked like he'd lost three inches and a week of sleep. His shoulders sagged as he pushed past her into the apartment. The work she'd been trying to catch up on had been interrupted by his text asking if he could come over.

She could never say no to him.

"Yeah. I just... We talked to our parents." He sat on the couch and stared into space.

It took Julie a moment to register who the 'we' was and what they had to talk about, but when it hit her she ran to his side and hugged him.

"Oh, Anthony. I'm so sorry. How did it go?"

He laughed, the sound forced and full of hurt.

"Exactly how I expected. They copped to it, and it just made me realize how selfish he'd been. No wonder my mom left."

Julie pulled back to see him, her fingers playing with the hair at the nape of his neck, thinking on how to respond. It didn't sound like any new information had come up, but she had never seen him quite like this before, so removed. She bit her lower lip.

"I'm sorry, babe. I guess it's good knowing for sure what happened, even if you'd already kind of known for the past few months."

"It's just so fucked, isn't it? Like, my mom left because my dad had an affair, but she looped me in with his mess and wanted nothing to do with me. My dad had an affair with his dead brother's wife, and didn't do anything to save the family he already had."

His eyes grew glassy, the wells at the brink of overflowing. Julie watched this man, this larger than life man, crack.

"How did you guys leave it?"

"I summarized the shit and walked out with Gideon. He's at Ella's. I don't know how to fix things."

Julie nodded and looked away. She didn't know

how to fix things either. Time was usually a factor, but having one parent completely walk out and another parent give up was complicated. But she realized that was almost the exact situation she was in with her own parents — and that, given enough time, she'd be ready to face them. Even if, ultimately, they could never be fixed.

"Well, take some time. You don't need to have an answer right now. You can stay here as long as you need." As soon as the words left her lips, Julie froze. "I— I'll be right back."

She jumped up and made her way down the hall. She'd left the door to the spare bedroom open, a member from the foster and adoption agency having come in earlier that evening for a home study and safety check. The last thing she needed to add onto this pile of shit was Anthony finding out about her foster plans. She'd tell him eventually, but tonight was not the night. Standing with her hand on the doorknob, she looked into the room, trying to see it from the eyes of the stern woman who'd made notes and asked questions. The woman, Marlene, had warmed up, even giving Julie a pity laugh for one of her corny jokes. She may be trying to single parent, but she had dad jokes aplenty. The room was as cozy and gender neutral as she could make it, and she hoped Marlene could see that where Julie lacked the support of a partner, she made up for with love. And a well-paying job. With a soft click, Julie closed the door.

Anthony was right where she'd left him, and he looked up at her as she padded into the living area.

"What can I do for you, Anthony?" She hoped her voice sounded more even than she felt.

He sighed. "I don't know. Could we just cuddle or something?"

"Of course." She went up to him and held him against her chest. He burrowed into her, lacing his arms around her waist and squeezing, shoulders rippling beneath her hands.

"How was your day?" It was muffled against her knit sweater.

Speaking of parents. "It was good. A day. I'm actually thinking of going home in a couple weeks."

Anthony pulled back, surprise written across his face. "Oh, really? How come?"

"I need to make things straight with my mom. It's time."

"I guess time can heal all wounds." He shrugged, pulling her onto his lap. "I can think of a few other things that might help."

Julie laughed as he started kissing her chest.

He wasn't wrong. There would always be some sort of issue to work through, but in the meantime, she might as well enjoy Anthony while she could.

16

"So I know we're supposed to be taking a break, but I have some news." Tom crossed his arms while he leaned against the sink, eyeing the band scattered about the apartment living room.

Anthony avoided his gaze. The floor was more interesting than that piece of shit, anyway.

"So The Strokes are touring next year, January to April, breaking in May before jumping into festival season. Their manager apparently saw one of our shows with Imagine Dragons, and they want us to open for them, January through April and June through August."

"That's great and all, but when are we going to headline our own shows?" Ryan asked from behind his raised soda can.

"Well, that's another thing. The label figures we'll have the third album done by spring and was planning on putting together a headliner show for the fall. So we need to figure out what schedule we want, if you guys want to be on tour for all or most of next year, and when you think we can get the next album done."

Almost a whole year? Anthony looked around the room, gauging everyone's reactions. Gideon looked less than thrilled. Ryan annoyed, Lucas and Max considering the options. Anthony's mind went to Julie. It'd been hard enough being away from her for six months. Worst case, he'd be in the studio with the guys almost every day for the next two or three months, then away for three or four. He'd have a month back with Julie, then be gone for another six.

He knew they could do it. He knew they could do anything. He just didn't want to be away from her for that long.

"This is some bullshit," Gideon muttered, pushing past Tom to the fridge. The other guys eyed one another.

"It's called being a musician," Tom said. "It's called working hard to get where we are. It's called having a little gratitude for all the opportunities you now have. Figure out what you guys want, I have a meeting."

Tom huffed through the living room, grabbing his coat and leaving with a slam.

Residual tension hung in the air, the spot on the ground more captivating than ever. When Anthony looked up, Lucas had his hands shoved in his pockets and Max was nodding his head to an internal beat. Ryan slurped his drink as Gideon slammed the fridge, soda in hand.

"So..." Anthony wanted to pretend that hadn't happened.

"So." Max looked around. "Not gonna ask what that was about, but we gotta figure out the tour schedule."

"Suit yourself, man." Ryan shook his head and turned to Anthony. "Is whatever's going on with you guys going to impact the band?"

Chewing his lower lip, Anthony hesitated. "I—I don't think so."

"It won't. Let's figure out this tour out." Gideon's tone was ice. "I vote we do all of it."

"I agree with Gid," Max said.

"Even though that basically means being in the studio or on the road for an entire year?" Ryan's confusion was evident in the cross of his brow.

"Dude, I don't even have a significant other, let alone a fiancée. I don't think Ella will be on board."

Gideon shrugged. "She'll be on tour with us anyway. But here's the thing — if we do all the tours this year, we can be picky moving forward. One more hard year for virtually a lifetime of freedom. We'll set ourselves up."

"Aren't we already set up?" Anthony hated where this conversation was going. "I mean, we toured with Imagine Dragons. That made The fucking STROKES want us."

"Why not split it? Do the January to April headline, skip festival season to work on our album, and come out strong in the fall with our own tour," Lucas said.

"Then when the fuck are we going to work on our album, if the label wants us to release in the spring?" Ryan's frustration was palpable; the rest of the band stood in silence, shifting their weight. Anthony had never seen Ryan like this before. Cocking his head, he eyed his friend and bandmate. He raised a valid point. They basically had two months to write, record, and release a new album if they joined the spring tour. And if they were going to split the dates, he'd rather do the spring tour than the festivals.

Anthony shuddered at the thought of doing another festival tour. Everything about them felt... dirty. The fields were always packed beyond reason, the smell of marijuana lingering in the air. More often than not, bands performed drunker than skunks. Considering Eternal Youths had three sober members — himself, Max, and Gideon, who Anthony worried was struggling — Anthony was hesitant to go another three months in that environment.

"Shit, sorry guys. I have to bounce." Max headed for the door. "I'm legit cool with whatever, just let me know."

"Same." Lucas trailed Max, shutting the door with a soft click behind him.

Anthony looked at Ryan and Gideon, both guys riled up and wanting very different things. He sighed. "Do you guys want to hash this out now or later?"

"Later. " Ryan shook his head and threw his empty soda can in recycling on his way out. "I'll catch you guys later."

In the wake of Ryan's absence, Anthony stared at the captivating spot on the floor.

"Yeah, I need to think. See you around, man." Gideon pushed past his cousin.

Anthony wasn't sure how long he stood in the empty kitchen for, his mind going a million miles a minute.

To tour or not to tour? For how long? What would Julie say?

Would Julie still be around if I was gone for a year?

17

Julie stared at the flight listings, the numbers jumbling into one. The girls in the office were chatting, distracting.

Holding her head in her hands, she reviewed the list again. Cheapest, fastest, shortest way to get home. To confront her mom about the blame of her sister's death. To hug her father and feel him slump against her in exhaustion.

Next week, early Tuesday morning. $80 and almost two and half hours. She'd return Friday afternoon. Julie didn't want to give her mom any more length of time to find a grudge. Three days was plenty.

She booked the ticket, thankful the others had quieted down. Julie glanced at Rachel's desk, her friend sitting with Ruby beside her. They were speaking in hushed tones and Ruby pointed to something on the computer. It'd been like this for the last week, Ruby and Rachel being close together and secretive. No matter how close Julie was with Rachel, she knew it was useless trying to dig for any information on what was happening. Ella would be in the same position; Rachel was a boss at separating her personal life from her work life. She'd never gossip about an employee with her two best friends.

Julie bit her lip. Rachel lived with their other best friend, Ben. There was a chance, however small, that Rachel talked to Ben about office life. But would it be seen as going behind Rachel's back to ask Ben?

Shit. Julie shook her head. The only reason she was so interested was because it involved Ruby. It had been over a year since Julie had left Anthony to travel the world, about eight months since she'd come home and found out he'd had a fling with her coworker. It was past time to let it go.

An incoming call popped up on her computer, the New York City area code the only familiar thing about it. Julie sent it to voicemail and texted her dad the flight information so he could pick her up.

Ruby laughed, causing a smile to crack on Rachel's smooth exterior. The pang of jealousy in

Julie's gut was gross — she knew better than to feel territorial over her friend. She shook her head, glancing at her phone. One new voicemail. She opened it, her eyes widening at the woman claiming to be from New York State's Office of Children and Family Services. Jumping from her desk, Julie left the office, trying to ignore the sudden hush and eyes following her out the door.

She replayed the message in the hallway.

"Hello Ms. Milligan, this is Jillian Buchanan with the Office of Children and Family Services. I'm calling in regards to your home visit. If you could please give me a call so we could set up an appointment, that would be great."

Ms. Buchanan recited her name and number several times. Or at least that's what it felt like, given how many times Julie replayed the message. She had to tamp down her excitement. This could be it, the call she'd been waiting for. But it could also be the call she dreaded, the one she rarely allowed herself to entertain.

How could anyone want a young, single woman to foster? How could they allow her to? Was her apartment set up appropriately?

There were moments in her life when her actions became fully realized. When it hit her how big, how grand, a decision was. This was one of those times.

"Jules?"

Ella's voice echoed in the concrete hallway, her hand soft as it laid on Julie's shoulder. Julie turned to her friend, blurred by tears.

"Oh my god, Julie, are you okay?"

She nodded. "The foster agency wants to meet. They left me a message. I either passed the apartment check or not. But they want to meet."

The look of horror on Ella's face disappeared into a smile as she pulled Julie into a tight hug.

Her best friend's arms wrapped around her, the tickle of Ella's hair against her face, the thump of her heart overtaking her anxiety.

Deep breaths.

This was happening.

Either way, this was real.

18

Anthony glanced at Julie, her hair pulled into a ponytail while she typed away at the dining table. Her apartment, while spacious, was still a small New York City apartment. The steam from the chicken stir-fry he was stirring over the stove filled the room, creating a haze beneath the overhead lights.

Julie had been working all night, trying to get ahead of her work before she went home for a couple days next week.

"Okay, sunshine. This is ready." Anthony turned off the stove and grabbed two bowls, filling them with rice and stir-fry before setting one beside her. He could barely make out her eyes behind the reflection of her blue-light glasses, but he knew they were glued to the screen.

"Hey, Jules?" He dipped his head down behind her laptop. "Jules?"

She glanced at him over the top of the screen, her face blank until it hit her he was there and food was ready by her elbow.

"Yes. Right. I'm so sorry. I'm done for the night, I promise." She shut the computer and took down her hair, combing the long blond strands with her fingers as she squeezed her eyes.

"Babe, it's okay if you need to keep working tonight. I just don't want your food to get cold and I think you could use a break, even if it's just twenty minutes."

"No, no. It's fine. I can finish up tomorrow, I still have a few days before I leave."

Anthony watched her body lengthen as she stood and stretched, smooth belly peeking out from below her tight thermal top, lush hips holding the waistband of her pajama pants from slipping. Her body leaned from side to side, arms reaching up as she groaned. She released the hold, her glasses slipping forward on her nose.

"What're you looking at, stud?"

Julie ambled towards him, grazing a hand along his bicep as she reached for a kiss. His lips met hers, his tongue pushing the petals open. He relished the taste of coffee and sunshine before she pulled away. Taking off her glasses, her eyes gazed into his.

"Want to watch something while we eat?"

Anthony hesitated. "I do, but I actually need to talk to you about the tour schedule for next year."

"Ah." She pursed her lips and grabbed one of the bowls on her way to the couch.

He followed, settling beside her. Anthony took in the set of her jaw, the slight flush in her cheeks. The way she avoided looking at him.

"So, we have a couple options and the band's taking time to think them through. First one is somehow find time to write, record, and release a new album, then open for The Strokes January through April and June through August, then run our headline tour September through December. Second option is open for The Strokes January through April, take a break during festival season, and then do our headline tour in the fall. Part of the problem is the label wants us to release a new album in the spring, so since it sounds like either way we'll be on tour January through April, we need to take the next two months to get the album done before then."

"And where are you guys leaning?" Julie's voice was soft. Tired.

"Well, Gideon and Max want to do it all. Ryan's just frustrated. Lucas wants to skip festival season in the summer, and I'm thinking that's probably the best option."

Julie barked out a laugh and shook her head. "Ella is not going to go for the all-in option. She'll do it, but she won't support it." She rested her head in her hand. "The festival skip sounds like the best option. So you won't really be around for the next year, I guess."

A sharp pain tore through Anthony's chest. The way she said it... The disappointment. The acceptance. The resignation.

Was this how his mom had felt about his dad being out, managing bands or doing who knows what?

He cleared his throat. "I'll be around the next couple months and in the summer."

Julie nodded.

"I know it sucks. And it'll be hard. But I'm not going anywhere." Anthony looked at her, wanting her to meet his gaze. To see how much he meant it when he said she would always be his home.

"But you are going. You'll always be going."

"And I'll always come back. And you'll be busy with work for a lot of that, and seeing your family and hanging with Rachel." He grasped for straws, trying to find ways to ease the pain. He remembered the edge of the guitar he'd seen in her spare bedroom. "And maybe some secret guitar practice? You wanna join Eternal Youths when we get back?" He hoped it'd make her laugh, but instead he was greeted with stiffness in her spine.

What the fuck was with that room?

Julie recovered with a small smile, throwing it his way. "Yeah, maybe."

"Jules. What's with the room?"

She rose and cleared their dishes. "What do you mean?"

"You know what I mean."

She was silent as she rinsed out the bowls and set them in the dishwasher.

"Julie, you get weird every time I mention it. You haven't offered to show it to me, even though you've shown me everything else in this place, from new paint to new cleaning supplies.

"It's just not ready, Anthony." She started putting the food away.

Anthony rose to meet her, setting his hands on her hips. His lips drifted to her neck.

"Just talk to me, Jules. What's going on? What are you hiding from me?"

"Nothing." She took a deep breath. "I just... I thought maybe you guys would be done with the whole year-long touring thing by now. And the on-and-off for three years, in-and-out thing isn't something I want. I need a bit more stability. Something constant. Something real."

She pulled away. Anthony stared at the counter while she moved behind him, the sound of water rushing through his ears.

Something real.

Something real.

"Do you — do you not think this is real?" The words, although in his voice, were separate from him.

"Of course I do," she said and sighed. "I know it's real. I'm just trying to figure out if it's meant to be more than what it is. And what I'm looking for."

Anthony turned to face her, crossing his arms across his chest. A pale armor to the barbs of her words launched out of left field.

"Well, it would help if you were honest with me. You hardly talk to me about work anymore, you keep an entire room in your apartment a secret. Now you're wondering if this is real?"

He watched the color rise in her cheeks, the volume of her voice echoing through the apartment.

"Oh, you mean the work where I have to sit across from the person you *fucked*? Good thing this *secret room* is in MY goddamn apartment. Good thing this apartment is even here otherwise you wouldn't have a place to go, would you? This is just easy. Easy for you to come and go, stay for however long you want and leave when you're ready."

Julie's words were ice, truth alongside anger. He saw it etched on her skin, raw in the clench of her jaw and the tears in her eyes. Anthony shook his head, disbelief at how this had devolved.

"I don't know what else to do to make you understand how much I love you." His voice was a whisper. "How much you're the one I want to be with, grow old with. I give you all I have. I don't know what else to do to make you happy, but if you're holding onto any of this shit, it's not going to work."

He pushed off the counter. A whiff of rose and vanilla assaulted him as he moved past his one and only love. Anthony slipped on his coat, throwing her one last look. A Rubenesque goddess trapped in her own restraints. She didn't meet his gaze.

The slam of the door behind him would haunt his dreams.

19

Julie stood in the kitchen, letting the slam of the door echo through her body.

Falling onto the couch, Julie stared at the closed door. Another closed door. She replayed their conversation, their fight, trying to find the points that had led to where they stopped. Coming up dry, she reached for her phone and sent the group chat an SOS. Ella, Rachel, and Ben would know what to do.

Julie curled up. Her mind buzzed, skin tingling with the realization Anthony had just... walked out. Walked away.

That she pushed him.

The buzz of the apartment intercom pulled her back to the room that seemed so much colder in the wake of Anthony. She wasn't sure how much time had passed.

"Hey, Jules."

Julie leaned against the door frame, clutching the front door knob as she stared at Ella in the hallway. Ella's rosy cheeks peeked out from her thick scarf, hair cascading in soft waves over her shoulders. She pushed her way into the apartment, unwrapping the various winter protection while saying something about Rachel coming later and Ben aiming to. Julie closed the door with a soft click before turning to face her friend.

"El, I don't know what to do."

Even Julie could hear the defeat laced in her own voice.

"No. No, you do know what to do. I don't know the deets — you're going to spill them now — but if I'm right about what I think the fight was about, then it's not a matter of not knowing. You're just scared to."

Ella refused to show her pity. With her jaw set, she started making tea. Julie knew this was what she needed, even if it stung. She filled Ella in on everything, from the tour to the room to the barbs she'd thrown at him. The words that sent him packing.

She grabbed her mug with the steeped liquid, avoiding Ella's gaze as she took a seat on the couch.

"So you lashed out because he was right." The couch sunk as Ella sat beside her friend. "And this is what I mean. You're scared to tell him your plans."

"But do you blame me? He's in and out. He stays here whenever he pleases, comes and goes at will. I don't think he factors me into his plans at all. Where is this supposed to go? There's no space for me and the life I want, there's only space for his touring."

A forced laugh came from the other side of the couch. "Seriously, Jules? First off, don't lash out at me," Ella said, shaking her head. "Secondly, it's not like you've opened up to him. It's not like you've actually, you know, *talked* to him about what you need and want and what your expectations are. If he's sensing you pulling away, or hiding things, of course he's going to react this way when you don't open up. Trust me, I've been there."

Ella shook her head and sipped her tea, the flush in her cheeks still visible through the steam. Julie clenched her jaw. She knew her best friend was right. Julie had given her the same advice when Ella was first dating Gideon. But there was a matter of not being open and there was a matter of seeing signs of something maybe not working long-term.

The problem was knowing the difference.

Julie sighed. "No, you're right. I know you're right. As much as I love him, as much as I want to be with him, if we don't want the same things then that's... that. But also, the signs are there. I think they've always been there."

She glanced at her friend, who was staring at her.

"Are you not even going to try and talk to him? Communicate what you need and want and give him the opportunity to do the same?"

"I don't really see the point if all the flags are there." Julie shrugged. "I mean, it's been on and off for three whole years. At what point is enough enough?"

"And at what point do you start to do the work to heal yourself and tear down those walls and let people in?"

"I have and I'm moving on."

Julie clenched her jaw, Ella blurring before her. She blinked away the tears, trying to blink away the obvious disappointment from her friend.

"Julie, I think this is a really big mistake."

"I know," Julie whispered.

"You're sure about these... these signs? Sure enough to let Anthony go?"

"I — Ella, it shouldn't be this hard. It's been three years and there's been no talk of what this looks like moving forward. But I *am* moving my life forward, and he's not fitting how I thought he would."

"It would help if you gave him a chance."

"It would help if he wanted it bad enough, if he'd say something."

"Hasn't he, though? Hasn't he given you the security you need to know what you have is real and he's in it for good? What more do you want from him?"

Julie sucked in a breath. Ella wasn't wrong — Anthony had always been vocal about her being the love his life, the one he wanted to be with forever. But saying was different than doing.

"I wanted him to put more action behind what he said. If I was really the one he wanted to be with, marriage would've come up. A discussion on what our careers would look like over the next year, how we could continue building what we started."

"Again, would you just *talk* to him? He could say the same thing to you." Ella's exasperation radiated between them.

"Ella, I shouldn't have to. You know it takes longer for guys to fall. If he wants something bad enough, he'll say it. He'll make it happen."

Ella snorted. "I think the shit you guys have been

through would be enough *action* behind everything he's told you. I really can't believe you're willing to do this. I know you're scared to really let him in. I know you're scared that now you're faced with the prospect of true love, a person to fully fold into your life, but you have to open up. I think you're being unfair and not giving him the chance he deserves. And you know that if you end it — for a second time, now — that it'll be done-r than done, right? There will be no coming back from this."

Julie let her words sink in. Maybe she was being unfair. Maybe she wasn't giving him a chance. She'd been alone for so long and never really had a relationship before. She'd always thought relationships should be easier than what she and Anthony had always had, that if a guy wanted something, he'd make it known. She'd always thought she'd be able to transition from being so individualistic to having a real partner. Julie hugged herself. Maybe she just wasn't who she thought she was.

Maybe she needed more obvious acts of security from Anthony in order to give him a chance.

Maybe she just wasn't ready for the things she wanted.

20

Anthony slapped his guitar strings, pacing while Gideon and Max went over a hiccup in their new song. Ryan plucked at the bass while Lucas turned his eyes to the ceiling, his foot tapping the bass drum pedal. Tom sat at a table against the far wall, by the door, staring into space.

There was an air in the practice room that weighed heavy, sealing Anthony in a bubble he didn't know how to leave. Eternal Youths had decided to record their next album before joining The Strokes' Winter/Spring Tour, and skipping festival season to rest up before their own headlining tour. But that meant pedal-to-the-metal writing and playing new music for the next few weeks.

He hadn't spoken to Julie since their fight a few

days ago. The stubborn streak that his father had bestowed upon him kept him from reaching out to her, and talking with Gideon had solidified his decision.

This wasn't the end, but he wasn't going to apologize. She could come to him.

It was only a matter of time. They needed to cool off. He'd been replaying their conversation since, and creating the next one in his head. She'd tell him she missed him, that they needed to talk. He'd go to her apartment, the door opening to her bright eyes and rose-scented skin. He'd envelop her, hold her, listen as she spilled everything and he forgave her.

"Ant?" Max's voice pulled him back to the room.

"Sorry," Anthony muttered. "What's the call?"

"We're going to start with the sax and on the 10th bar, Gideon's going to come in. We're pushing you to the drop halfway, when the gospel singers come in." Max fingered his saxophone, glancing at each of the guys. They nodded and settled in, starting the revision.

Anthony had some time before his entrance, and he tried to imagine the gospel singers incorporated in their indie rock song. Since Gideon — their main songwriter — had gotten sober and engaged, their sound had evolved from melancholy coffee house rock to something almost fun and ethereal. The sax had become a defining aspect, changing the melancholy to bittersweet and sometimes sultry. Now the gospel singers would hit on that in this particular song, and would reprise their role at the end of the album with the same words, but... happier? That was the gist Anthony got from the way Max and Gideon explained it.

"Seriously?"

Ryan stopped the band, and when Anthony looked at him, his normally fair skin was cherry-red.

Oh. He'd been the one who stopped the band. He hadn't even joined them.

"Sorry." Anthony sighed and plucked the strings. "Go again?"

The band grumbled but reset. Anthony tried listening to the soulful blare of the sax, but its call only brought him back to a time when he'd been making dinner Julie's apartment. Miles Davis was on in the back and her arms snaked around his waist, pulling him into a sway in the middle of the living room. He closed his eyes against the softness of her hair, the tenderness of her arms holding him to her heart. Hindsight was twenty-twenty, and Anthony realized that might be the closest he'd ever truly been to the Juliette hidden behind walls of ice and stone.

"Anthony, dude. What the fuck." Lucas pulled back on the drums, and the room went silent.

Anthony had done it again.

"Shit, guys. I'm sorry." He rubbed his face, ran his hand through his hair. Placed his fingers on the cold, thin strings of the guitar. "Okay. Ready?"

Ryan scoffed, Max chewed his lower lip, Gideon stared at the ground.

"Look, man," Lucas said, "we know there's a lot going on with the tour and Julie and shit, but could you focus? The sooner we get this done, the sooner we can move on." Exasperated, he fixed his bun, a souvenir from the band's beginning that he refused to shave off to match the bare sides.

Anthony froze. "How do you know about Julie?" He'd only spoken to Gideon about that. He looked at his cousin, who shifted on his feet.

Lucas glanced at the other guys, his jaw clenching as he turned back to Anthony. "Dude, anytime anyone's off, it's always about a girl. Can we get back to this?"

Anthony stared at Lucas before nodding and glancing at Gideon. Gideon's back was turned, head down while his hand moved along the neck of his guitar.

That fucker had talked. Betrayed his confidence.

The anger rose through his body, his skin turning hot.

"You know what? Figure it out without me." Anthony put the guitar on a stand and stormed between the guys. The door called him, and shoving past his dad was only cathartic. He needed to clear his head. It was one thing to be in a room full of people you loved.

It was another to know how utterly alone you were.

21

Julie looked over at her dad, a sad smile creeping across her face. His bald head shone in the sun as they drove to the house from O'Hare, his face soft and tired. She hadn't realized how much she'd missed him until he'd wrapped her in a bear hug, his big frame showing her own that sometimes, she didn't have to be the one to stand so tall.

They reached the more residential neighborhoods, and as they neared Julie's reckoning, she counted the houses in her head.

Mary. Sam. Melissa. Jackson.

Kids who were no longer wrapped in the adolescent skin she'd once known. Kids who'd gone and come back and left again or stayed, raising their own families amid the debris of the ones they'd grown up in.

Julie sighed, her mind trailing to the life she now lived. The man she once thought she'd grow old with. The strength and sacrifices everyone made to keep a small portion of love and happiness. To her own parents, who'd made their way through jobs and kids and horror and laughter.

When, how, did you know to keep fighting? To let go?

"Honey bear."

Carty's soft voice called from the driver's seat, the tan ranch house before them. The only house Carty and Karen Milligan had ever bought and raised their family in. Julie knew her mom was inside, either puttering in the kitchen or crocheting on the couch in the living room. Julie took a deep breath and glanced at her dad.

"It'll be okay. I promise," he said. "She knows you're coming, and she knows it's time for you guys to have a real, honest-to-God conversation." His hand rested on her shoulder. "And you know I'm always here for you." He gave it a little squeeze before stepping out of the car. He made it to the front porch before he realized she hadn't followed, stopping to wait for her.

It was now or never.

Julie hauled her bag over her shoulder and joined her dad. She gave him a quick side hug before they entered the building, immediately greeted with the white couches of the family room no one ever used. They all preferred the living room tucked away in the back of the house, by the backyard.

As partially expected, the sound of pots clanging and whistling tea kettle flowed through the house. Carty gave Julie one more shoulder pat before heading into the kitchen, becoming hidden by the wall. Julie heard their murmurs with the stop of pots and tea kettles. She slowly walked past the hidden kitchen, down the hall and into her bedroom. She could always count on her parents' keeping everything the exact same.

She knew the closed door across from hers still bared the scars of an eleven-year-old's stuffed animals, left behind with half-finished homework and aged photos of long-lost friends.

Julie set her bag on the bed and looked at her own memorabilia. Any changes over the years had been her own. After Hannah's death, she'd thrown out anything that had reminded Julie of her sister. She felt a pang in her heart at the loss of the toys they'd shared and the secrets they'd kept. The stuffed animal they'd marked with red ink, a case of the chicken pox keeping the lion from her tea party when Hannah was five. The expensive doll whose hair they cut when Hannah was eight, not knowing it would't grow back and hiding it under the bed until the trash bag sealed the doll's future. The diary Julie used to keep, the one with a lock Hannah had learned to pick just a few months before the accident.

After the trash bag, Julie had kept her room sparse. She'd painted the walls a white to match the oppression she felt and then called it a day. She was too busy getting her grades even higher, her scholarships even more fruitful. Doctor or lawyer, doctor or lawyer. Anything to make her parents happy. Once college hit, she'd cleaned out her favored objects to take with her. Post-college, she'd left a few bins of unneeded items beneath the bed. Julie didn't need to check to know they were still there, begging to be released.

Another trash bag for another day.

"Juliette?"

Julie whipped around at the sound of her mother's voice from her doorframe.

Karen's blonde hair hung limp around her face, more tired than usual. Defeated. Her hands looked knotty, as though the years of crocheting her anxiety away were finally catching up. Her ice blue eyes skittered across Julie's bare room, refusing to meet their mirror. Julie had gotten her eyes from her mom; she knew how unsettling it was to see yourself in someone you ached to love but who stood in a prison of their own making.

Julie shifted her weight and crossed her arms. It was easy to feel young in the presence of a parent. Especially when they had so much to come to terms with.

"Hi, Mom."

"Did you have a nice flight?" Karen cleared her throat. "I made tea. It's in the kitchen but I can bring it here if you like."

Julie hugged herself and looked around the room. If she and her mom were going to get into it, she wanted to be comfortable.

"Let's go into the living room."

22

Anthony paced outside of the building. He'd made it as far as the parking lot before seeing Ryan's van and realizing he couldn't actually leave, not with his wallet and phone in the pocket of his winter coat still inside the practice room. Ryan was usually their driver, and the back of that van had been a home in more ways than one, many a time. His dad had arrived separately, but he couldn't see the car and there was no way in hell he was going to ride alongside that piece of shit.

He'd have to wait for his pissed-off bandmate to come out.

Or he could get out of the December cold he wasn't appropriately dressed for, head back to the room and finish what they'd started.

He laughed to himself.

Yeah, right.

Going back would put his tail between his legs, and that was not the ending to his stomp-off he was willing to accept. His cousin had clearly talked to the guys about the fight with Julie, something Anthony wasn't ready to share with the others. Not until he knew where he and Julie stood.

Not until he knew where he stood.

The cold was biting through the thin zip-up hoodie, his blood boiling with anger at his cousin and at Julie. Anthony had never felt more alive.

The door to the building opened with a groan, the heavy footsteps ones he would always be able to recognize.

"Anthony, come on."

Tom stood — appropriately dressed — with his arms crossed over Anthony's coat. It was the most he'd spoken to his son in weeks, following the destruction of their own relationship. No thanks to Tom, but still.

He had followed Anthony.

He had come.

"Anthony, what's going on?" His dad edged closer, arm holding out the peace offering.

The fire in Anthony climbed to his eyes. He turned around and blinked back the sting of tears.

The heavy footsteps turned to a shuffle behind him, the hard wool of his coat pushing against his shoulder. The salt stung his frozen cheeks as the tears made their escape south, and Anthony tried to keep the wracking of his shoulders from totally depleting his exterior armor. He may be upset, but he'd learned from the best that it was better to hide it. He couldn't show his teacher he'd failed.

"Bud, why don't we go sit in the car."

The use of his childhood nickname sent Anthony spinning, his shoulders shaking. He let his dad lead him to the back of the building where the black Altima sat. They climbed in, Tom sitting in silence while Anthony emptied himself. Of Gideon, of his mom. Of the terror and possibility of losing Julie but not knowing how to move forward. Of refusing to be a sucker for a woman but unable to pull himself out of her orbit.

Exhausted, Anthony leaned forward, his body settling into a rhythmic shake that was seeing itself out. He took a few deep breaths. He'd always felt better after a good release. It used to be found at the bottom of a bottle. Then it was in the comforting solitude of his empty apartment in Sugar Grove. Never in his life did he expect to find it in the car beside his dad, let alone during a time when he hadn't realized he'd already forgiven his dad for his faults.

Anthony gathered his bearings while the silence filled the small space.

"I'm sorry. For everything. But especially for hiding. Hiding what I did, hiding how I felt, hiding parts of mine and your mom's relationship from you. I'm just... I'm so sorry."

Anthony looked at his dad, who stared forward.

Tom didn't apologize. Rarely, if ever.

"Look," Tom turned to his son. "Your mom and I kept a lot from you. We thought we were protecting you. Our marriage was over long before it ended. Yes, my affair with Amelia had a part in that. There's no excuse for my behavior, even though I spent years feeding every excuse I could find to your mom and to myself. But sometimes you reach a point where it's not healthy to keep fighting. Sometimes you both stop fighting, sometimes one has been fighting longer, harder, than the other. But only the individual can make that call. I'm not really sure what to say about you and Julie. I've never seen you so happy with someone before, and I have no doubt you do the same for her. But the lack of communication, the lack of understanding, is a bit of a deal breaker."

Tom sighed. "Honestly, Ant? I think one of the biggest issues anyone can have is too much pride. I think what you and Julie have is more special than most. Maybe it's run its course. Maybe it hasn't. But if you have too much pride, I worry you won't find out which one it is."

Anthony met his dad's gaze. To hear him open up, even a little bit, about his relationship with his mom was one thing. It was another for Tom to give him his thoughts, his advice. Anthony mulled over what he said.

"I've already fought for our relationship, though."

"And? Hasn't she also fought for it?"

"Yeah. She's also been the one to break it before. If she breaks it again, isn't it time to move on?"

A sad chuckle escaped Tom. "Boy, you guys will continue to break it. There will be times when you argue and cry and break each other's hearts. That's a given. It's a matter of what's worth it to you, and what's healthy. The secrecy isn't healthy, but neither is the not talking. Neither of you have ever really been in a relationship before. I think instead of continuing to be on and off, it's time to sort it out. Whatever will be, will be. Que sera, sera."

Anthony smiled at the song reference. His mom would hum it while getting him ready for school. He couldn't remember when she stopped the ritual, only that she had.

"What about Gideon?" His cousin betraying his trust gnawed at him.

"What about Gideon? He's your cousin. Stop hiding and talk to him, too. He probably needed a friend and didn't know who to turn to. No excuse, but get the story straight before you attach yourself to an outcome that probably doesn't need to exist." Tom's phone buzzed, and he typed out a quick text before buckling his seatbelt. "The guys are done sorting out the next few songs, so they're calling it a day. Let's go home, and you can sort yourself out."

Anthony pulled the belt across his chest, clicking the piece into place. He really just wanted to nap. The sorting could come after, especially since Julie would be home in Chicago for the next few days.

But maybe a quick text to her wouldn't hurt.

23

Julie settled into the couch in the living room, setting her tea mug on the glass coffee table. Her mom sat at the other end, her dad's recliner remaining empty. She could almost hear his snoring, despite the empty napping spot.

The brown couches in the living room were infinitely more comfortable than the white leather ones in the family room at the front of the house. The family room was a strange entryway that melded with the dining room, sitting across from the kitchen on the left. Between the kitchen and the dining room sat the entryway into the living room, where the family typically relaxed. Julie didn't know how to start this conversation, but she knew she wanted to do it where she could feel her dad's presence, his strength, even if he wasn't physically there.

Karen cleared her throat, her gaze roaming the room. She took a deep breath. Steeling herself. She met Julie's eyes.

"Yes, I do — did — blame you for Hannah's death." She fingered the silver chain around her neck, the one that once carried a silver cross. "Now, you know I don't like confrontation. But your father insisted we talk, so here we are."

Julie knew to expect some sort of pushback. What she didn't expect was her mom to outright own the wedge that had made itself a home between them. She could only blink at her mom, balancing the admission against Karen's unwillingness to take responsibility.

"Will you say something?" Karen's voice shook.

"Seriously?" Julie couldn't believe her ears. "What would you like to me to say? Oh, gee, thanks, *Mom,* for admitting you blame me for the death of your daughter? Thanks for forcing yourself to sit here because it would make Dad happy? Wow." Julie shook her head and leaned back against the couch. The familiar pressure provided some comfort.

Karen laughed. "I knew it would be like this. God forbid you take any responsibility."

"Are you kidding me right now? Responsibility for what? A DRUNK RAN A RED LIGHT!"

"And you were the one driving through a yellow. You should've stopped."

Julie felt the heat in her cheeks as she took what little hope for a conversation and turned it into a shouting match. She'd been expecting tears to brim, but found herself more tired and angry than anything. When it came to her mom, Julie must've cried out everything she'd held onto.

"But how is that my fault?" Julie tried lowering her voice, but it still raised to a fever pitch. "How can you possibly find fault in that? I followed the laws of the road. I checked both ways, I slowed down. I'm sorry your daughter died, but I lost a sister. She died right next to me. I saw it happen. I WAS THERE."

The words came out in a rush. Breathless, Julie realized what she'd said. What she'd pushed away from her memories in a sorry attempt to move on. She had seen everything. It had happened in slow motion, like in a movie. She'd always thought that was a silly notion, something to make trauma relatable. No matter what that trauma was, everyone could see it like a movie.

Separate. Unreal.

But the smile on Hannah's face being greeted by

the grill of a black pickup truck as it rammed into her side, pushing her closer in one way but farther in others from Julie, wasn't separate. It wasn't unreal.

That smile had been her last *I love you*.

Her laugh had been her last *I forgive you*.

Julie had woken up in the hospital, her head throbbing from the impact of a window that refused to break while her heart did the shattering, her parents toppled over in puke-green chairs.

Separate. Untouching.

The memory had lived in the dark part of Julie's brain, the part she knew her body had tried to cover up. It only revealed itself, barely, when a car stopped too fast. She let it live out now that she had pulled it from the quicksand, let it live out in the horror of her mother's ice blue eyes that refused to fill with tears.

Julie took a shaky breath, knowing her mother would never be the one to breach this silence. "I know I was the one driving when it happened. I know you may always, always hold part of me responsible. Maybe if you'd been driving, you wouldn't have driven through the yellow. Maybe you would've. Maybe if you'd been driving, you wouldn't have stopped for ice cream before coming home. Maybe you would've. But I'm tired of maybe, Mom. Aren't you?"

Karen stared at her daughter. The last piece of herself.

"I don't know how to live without it. Without her." It came as a whisper, laced with fear.

Her mom was scared. Scared of a life where Hannah wasn't a ghost around every corner. A life where blame could lay in pictures throughout the house, in a skin that matched her own with familiar eyes that carved paths through glaciers.

An overwhelming sadness settled over Julie. Her mother hadn't been blaming Julie for Hannah's death.

Karen had been blaming herself.

It was easier to blame yourself through someone that resembled you, but wasn't you. Someone that had been at the scene of a crime, had seen those last moments, when you hadn't. Julie swallowed the lump in her throat. All these years, she'd thought she'd been the strong one by cutting Hannah out completely. But it had been her mom, who needed the forgotten promise of her younger daughter in order to stand straight, to walk down halls and into rooms and continue as if that promise would still one day be filled. Karen woke every day to face that empty promise.

"Mom, I promise you she will always be here. I

tried to pretend it didn't happen, and look where I am. There has to be a middle ground, but I don't think we'll find it separately."

Karen bowed her head, hiding the way her face turned splotchy when she cried. Her slim shoulders shook with the releasing weight, and Julie scooted next to her mom, who felt so small in her arms. She was built like Hannah and felt like she had.

Julie closed her eyes at the thought. "I think it's okay to think about Hannah without pretending she'll walk through the door. That's not a maybe. But we have each other. We've always had each other."

"I — I think," her mom hiccuped. "I think part of it is, I was planning on taking her for ice cream after practice. I should've been the one driving. But Grandma called and needed help, so I asked you to pick her up. A— And I could've lost both of you." Her sobs echoed through the room, muffled against the tired skin of her hands. Julie hadn't realized how far down the guilt ran.

"Mom, have you... you know, talked to anyone? Not just Dad, but, like, a therapist?"

The hiccups coming from her mom slowed. "Juliette, I've never talked to anyone about this. I — I think your father caught on. God never listened."

Her laugh was hard before returning to tears. "What was I to do?"

The apple didn't fall far from the tree.

"You know, I never talked to anyone either. I didn't even tell anyone I had a sister until last year. I was so angry I threw out everything I had that we shared. What was I to do? I threw everything out, and you kept everything. But we were both hurt, and we were both grieving, and we both took it out on one another."

Her mom shook her head, wiping her face. "Oh, honey. We knew what was in that trash bag. It's in the attic." Karen looked at Julie and started laughing.

Julie couldn't believe it. The way her mom had been haunted was the very thing that had saved Julie's one regret.

"In the attic?"

"In the attic." Her mom took a deep breath, allowing the tears to fall. "I know it's time. It's past time. I just don't know where to start."

"I think we pick a place and we just... start. We. Not I, or you, or Dad. We. And we cry and we laugh and we remember and we let go."

Her mom nodded and hugged Julie. "Thank you. You were the only thing keeping me going, all those years. I'm sorry for not being the mom you needed,

Juliette. You'll do far better than me if the time ever comes."

Julie smiled at the comment. It went far deeper than her mom could know in this moment. Julie was used to seeing those digs as thorns. But knowing the full story, she saw her mom had always acted out of fear. She had been scared Julie would turn out like her.

"Mom, you were exactly what and where you needed to be. It sucked, but I am who I am because of it all. And I wouldn't change any of that. I love you, and I forgive you."

24

The text Anthony shot off to Julie in the car had gone unanswered, and he tried to not let it get under his skin. He knew she was dealing with her own parental shit. She probably didn't want to hear from him.

The door buzzed with Gideon's arrival. Anthony let the butterflies in his stomach escape. He didn't know why he was nervous, but he was. He couldn't imagine what his cousin would use an excuse for betraying his confidence. Anthony didn't give a flying fuck that the people Gideon had told were practically brothers.

"Hey." He opened the door and shuffled back to the kitchen, popping a bottle of ginger beer while Gideon took off his shoes and coat in the apartment entryway. Anthony left one for Gideon on the counter and took a seat on the couch. He listened to Gideon grab the bottle, his heavy steps softened by the carpet in the living area. The couch bowed with his weight as he sat beside Anthony.

"How you doing, Ant?"

Anthony sipped his brew, not for the first time wishing it was something stronger. He hated these kinds of conversations. He didn't look at his cousin.

"Well, Gid, I'd be doing a lot better if I knew why the rest of the band knew there was something up with me and Julie."

Gideon sighed. "I'm sorry. I — I don't know, I just needed to talk to someone. You and Julie have your problems but I never thought it'd be this bad, ya know? I always read you guys like me and Ella. And if you guys are in trouble... Well, what does that say about my relationship?"

Anthony mulled over Gideon's words. His cousin was rarely straightforward and had a habit of greeting conversations with anger. But he'd remained calm, cool. Collected.

"Being engaged does wonders for you." Anthony practically spit the words out before taking another sip. The ginger burn was just enough to soothe his tongue while making him miss the sting and loosening power of whiskey.

"Dude, what's that supposed to mean?"

"It means you've gotten nicer since popping the question."

Gideon laughed. "Yeah, I have. Being in a real relationship where you talk about your problems and hopes and dreams really sets shit straight. You should try it instead of being angry that I have something you want."

"Well, I'm trying to right now. Why the fuck would you talk to everyone about my shit? Why didn't you just talk to me."

"Because you won't listen. The fight you had was never finished — you walked off. I was frustrated and needed to talk to someone. So I talked with Max and Ryan, and one of them must've told Lucas. That's it. That's the story."

"How can you say the fight was never finished? She said she didn't know if what we had was real. Here I was planning on our future together, and she didn't even see it existing."

"Anthony, you have to actually, you know, *talk* to her about your future together." Gideon shook his head. "You're a piece of work, you know that?"

"I'm just tired. I feel like I'm always the one to mend things. To bring things up. She's the one that takes off. That hides. And it's exhausting." Anthony sighed.

"I get that. Seriously. Ella and I had plenty of issues with secrecy and letting each other in. But you gotta talk about this stuff, man. You need to articulate what's a problem and what you're willing to live with and what you're not."

Anthony took another swig from his drink. The initial onslaught of the conversation was over, the butterflies settling. "Still no excuse to share my private life with people. Even if it is the band."

"You're right, and I apologized. Won't happen again. But if you could work on these conversations not turning into heated attacks, that'd help your cause a lot."

"Gotta keep you on your toes."

"Right, if that's what you call it." Gideon snorted. "So... When will you talk to her? She's at her parent's, right?"

Anthony tapped his bottle. "Yeah, that's a whole thing. I texted her yesterday but she hasn't responded yet."

Gideon nodded. "Might take some time. Hell, you had to go to rehab and I fell off the wagon before. We all have our shit. She probably just needs a little space. But she'll come back."

Anthony stared at his bottle, his cousin's words sliding right through him.

She might come back.

There was no way to tell Gideon how much he needed her to.

He'd put everything on the table. One last Hail Mary.

She had to come back, but it'd be the last time he'd turn himself in knots for her.

25

Julie stared at her phone screen, Anthony's text staring right back at her. Asking to talk. Asking for a no-holds-barred, put all the cards on the table kind of talk. She chewed her lower lip. She'd hurt him — more than once — and he'd finally left.

But he came back.

The pit in her stomach helped in her slump down the bed, until she was facing the ceiling. The phone laid facedown on her stomach while she tried to steady her breathing.

He deserved better, and she knew it.

Julie had always felt that people would rise to her expectations. And when they didn't... Well, she knew how to let the door hit them on the way out. So why couldn't she hold herself to the same standard?

Anthony deserved not only the truth, but a woman, a partner, who could face him with every doubt, every dream, every need. Just like she expected of him.

Her mom's laugh carried from the kitchen. Julie smiled. It'd been years since her mom had openly laughed in this house, at least when Julie was around. The heavy blanket Hannah had stitched over their roof was finally unraveling, the suffocating wool being replaced with lace. It'd been two says since their big talk, and they'd had several smaller talks since. Some with Carty, some without. Some with tears, some with yelling, some with laughter. Some with all three. But they always ended with a hug. *I love you. I forgive you.* They knew their wounds wouldn't heal overnight, not with the way they were embedded in their bones. But they could start.

They'd started clearing out Hannah's room the day after The Big Talk. Caressing clothes and stuffed animals, kissing favorite books before placing them in a box, hopeful to pass them along to grandchildren. Julie had yet to tell them her plans — she didn't need the judgements or questions right now. But she did tell them about Anthony. Only the good stuff, but still.

It was a start.

For the first time in her life, Julie felt peace. On track.

Life was made of new starts if she was willing to see them.

Maybe she and Anthony just needed another one in order to move forward together.

After she sent her response agreeing to talk to him and giving him her timetable, she joined her parents in the kitchen. Carty dropped a kiss on Karen's forehead before leaving for the living room, a new book in hand. Julie couldn't remember the last time they'd been affectionate in front of her. Lately, she could hear their hushed voices through their closed door, late into the night. Sometimes there were bouts of silence, sometimes slightly raised voices until they remembered that, for once, they weren't alone.

"Hey, honey," her mom asked. "Want some tea?"

"Please." Julie smiled and watched her mom flit about, pulling mugs and tea bags while the water boiled. She still seemed older than what Julie remembered from her last visit, but there was something about Karen that felt more open than before. Brighter.

"When are you leaving again?" her mom asked.

"I should head out tomorrow. While I have some leniency with work, I don't want to push it."

"I don't know if I ever asked you what you do, not since..."

Julie knew her mom was leaving off the time Julie had come home for the ten year anniversary of Hannah's death last year. There'd been a brief conversation on how she did the contracts for her friends' company, but it'd been cut short by one of her mom's barbs. Her mom was a retired administrative assistant — of course she'd be nervous her daughter's law degree was going to waste at a start-up.

"Well... I actually head up their nonprofit division now." Julie cleared her throat, waiting for the attack.

"Oh! Oh. That's amazing, Juliette. What... What do you do?" Her mom slid a mug of tea over and sat on one of the barstools under the peninsula between them.

Julie tried to hide her shock but was sure she was unsuccessful by her mom's laugh.

"Honey, I just want you to be happy. Are you happy?"

Who was this alien?

"I — Yeah. Yeah, mom, I am." Julie cocked her

head and looked at her mom, who was staring at her in earnest.

"So you run the nonprofit part. What do you do?"

"I'm the head of it, so... everything. We're focusing on rehabilitating domestic abuse survivors, providing child care to at-risk youth, and providing after-school programs. Not just for tutoring, but for creative outlets. So right now I'm focusing on fundraising and awareness while we search for volunteers who are licensed in the fields we need. And eventually, depending on the fundraising, we would outright hire those certified. But before that, we would purchase a property we could outfit to house, tutor, and provide the child care. It'll be the Maven Media headquarters, so it would double as an office space as well as a shelter. Eventually we'll add programs for the parents or single parents in domestic abuse and poverty situations, but that's down the line." Julie stopped short of telling her mom about the financial advisement, self-care, and stress management classes they hoped to offer parents, as well as the ultimate dream of setting individual parents up with a mentor, a counselor, to help them get on their feet in their second life.

Baby steps.

"I'm... I'm so proud of you." Karen's eyes filled, her words cutting into Julie.

Proud.

That's all she ever wanted from her mom. All it took was traveling the world to 'find' herself. All it took was seeing that strength was in doing what she wanted instead of what she thought everyone wanted for her.

"How are you building awareness?" Her mom's question pulled her back to the little kitchen.

"We're reaching out to various shelters to see how big the need is. We're also going to be talking to different city officials and psychologists about the best way to reach people actively in those situations, who have yet to leave."

"How are you making sure those people won't get lost in the shuffle?"

"How do you mean?"

"Well, when I worked at the college, the goal was to, and forgive me for the phrasing, 'capture' people. How do we hook them and keep them coming back? Are you running any sort of volunteer programs currently to start building that trust with the shelters and occupants?"

Julie cocked her head. She'd never given her mom much credit. An administrative assistant for the dean had always sounded like a secretary, and from the stories her mom used to tell, it mainly consisted of emails, calendars, and phone calls. But when she thought about working at Maven Media, she realized that virtually everyone — no matter the department — eventually had a say in some of the broader aspects of the company.

Especially when it came to outreach.

"I didn't realize you had a hand in marketing, mom. We don't run programs like those, but I'm open to any ideas."

Karen smiled. "Oh, boy, do I have some. I may have worked for a college, but being a mom was my favorite job."

Julie pulled out the barstool opposite her mom and sat. She sipped her tea, thankful for the excitement she saw in her mom's face, the way she waved her hands, her eyes big. Thankful that, after all this time, they could still have a relationship.

26

"Good evening, Carl."

Anthony's hand was sweating around the bouquet of flowers. He nodded at Julie's elder neighbor as the man shuffled out of the ancient elevator. He was greeted with a lopsided smile and a shaky wave. The man's other hand was barely holding onto a cane.

That was new.

"You doing okay?" Anthony had had several encounters with Carl, and with each one he grew to love the old man like the grandfather he never had.

"Eh, you know how it is. One day you feel on top of the world, the next you're on the floor of it. Literally." He chuckled. "Just took a little fall a few weeks ago. Things don't work like they used to. You going to see Miss Juliette?"

Anthony smiled at the name. "Yes, I am. Want me to tell her anything?"

Carl shook his head. "Not really. Now I know it's none of my business, but no one should yell as loud as she did last week. And neither should you. I hope you have a good rest of your day." He tipped his hat and shuffled past Anthony, who barely gathered himself together in time to step aside, careful to keep the flowers from being squished in the shuffle. His cheeks heated at the thought of the kind man hearing their row a few nights ago.

"You, too," Anthony muttered. But Carl was already on the sidewalk, looking side to side as the door shut with a soft click behind him.

Onwards and upwards.

Normally Anthony felt loving butterflies when he entered Julie's building, and normally run-ins with Carl were filled with jokes and laughter.

Not this time.

The mood was already soured. Anthony knew this conversation was going to be big. He knew there was no clear ending, no timeline. Just his heart on the line.

And hers.

He swallowed and raised his hand to knock on Julie's door, but she opened it before he got the chance. His sharp breath gave him away, but he would never not be in awe of her. In awe of the way her velvet lips parted when she saw him, calling to his. In the soft cascade of gold on her shoulders, begging to be tucked behind her ear. In the flush of her cheeks, rosy and truthful. She crossed her arms over her chest, a small smile playing at the corners of her lips.

"You're ridiculous," she mumbled, turning to let him in. Anthony couldn't help his gaze drift to her luscious butt in those tight yoga pants.

He had no doubt she knew what to wear to disarm him, even though she should know her voice was enough.

"Thanks for coming, Anthony."

Disarming even when she sounded formal.

"Of course, sunshine. I — I brought you these." He blushed and handed the flowers out, feeling like a sixteen-year-old on his first date. Julie uncrossed her arms and pulled the stems to her, closing her eyes as she breathed them in. Roses, sunflowers, tulips.

"They didn't have marigolds. I know how much you love those." Anthony shoved his hands in his pockets and rocked back and forth. He may or may not have traipsed through all of the East Village, the West Village, and most of Midtown looking for the sunset orange flowers Julie had fallen in love with — in their brightness and strength and humility — when she was in India.

"Anthony, they're beautiful. Thank you so much." She pecked him on the cheek, the assault of her vanilla and rose-scented skin forcing his eyes closed. He wanted to live in that dream forever. His hand found its way to her hip before she pulled away, the moment gone. She busied herself with putting the flowers in a vase. Silent.

Not a *great* sign.

But he wanted her to start. He understood his dad's talk about pride, but Anthony had texted her first. He had found his way here. To her apartment. He'd brought her flowers. He'd brought her himself. She could start the conversation.

When she was done arranging the flowers, she left the finished product on the counter and turned to him.

"So."

"So."

"Anthony... I'm sorry about the other night. I do know this is real. I said it in the heat of the moment, but you're the only one I've ever loved and the only one I want to be with."

"I feel like the 'drunk words are sober thoughts' thing applies to heat-of-the-moment situations. What part of you feels like we aren't real?" Anthony wanted to run, to tap his foot, to pace. Literally anything but stand in the ache of their honesty.

Julie looked at the floor before standing straighter and meeting his gaze. "I love you, but I need to know where this is going. Not just us — " she motioned between them, "but you, specifically. What do you want? Where do you see yourself in the next year? Three?"

Anthony couldn't help the chuckle from escaping. "Is this a job interview?"

"This isn't funny. Because yeah, in a lot of ways, it is a job interview. I love you but... but if our time is up, I'd rather just know."

Well, that was sobering.

Anthony cleared his throat. "Okay. Um. Yeah. Okay. Can we sit?" At least sitting would allow him to tap his foot or something.

"I'd rather not."

He shoved his hands in his pocket and played with the apartment keys. It was better than nothing. He'd been preparing for this moment for days, going over it with his dad and Gideon until his mouth dried and his ears heard the words in his sleep. An actor embedding his lines in his being, for fear of stage fright.

So much for preparation.

Anthony swallowed. If Julie had planned on disarming him, she'd done a great job. Between her physical closeness, those pants, and her knowing him so well as to not let him sit, Anthony was lost. But he knew his truth — that hadn't needed any practice.

"I want to marry you, Juliette Milligan." He watched her face as she took in a sharp breath, her arms tightening across her chest. "In the next year, I see me coming back from tour and staying put. In three years, I see us welcoming our first child. Julie, I'm tired of everything being about the band all the time. I want room for you. But most of all, I need you to make room for me. No more secrets. No more lies, no matter how little they are."

Anthony wasn't sure how long she'd stared at him, but when she finally spoke, it was barely above a whisper.

"I need to show you something."

27

Julie could barely hear her own footsteps over the sound of her thumping heart as she led Anthony down the hallway.

One foot in front of the other.

In a minute, everything would be on the table.

He'd either leave or he'd stay.

His steps behind her were tentative, and when she reached the door that hid her dreams, he stopped once his chest was pressed against her back. His big, hard, broad chest that she'd spent hours memorizing. The hills and valleys her fingertips had caressed, the patterns her tongue drew across the flat planes. Her home lay just behind that chest, thumping in time with his home in her. Julie leaned against him, wanting that last pillar of comfort, before taking a shaky breath and opening the door.

They stepped through, and she watched her reformed bad boy tour the room, fingering its contents. Guitar. Books. Art supplies. Bed. He turned to her, mouth open and hair falling across his forehead. She stopped herself from reaching up to push the stray lock aside. His blue eyes were dark in a way she'd never seen.

"I applied to be a foster parent when you were on tour last summer." The words came out in a rush, becoming the wind beneath her sails. "I realized after volunteering in India that I wanted nothing more than to help kids, and that was able to manifest at Maven Media. But something was still missing, and I realized that all this time I'd been running away from my own mom because I couldn't do anything to make her happy and I didn't want to be like her. But then I thought more about it, and it wasn't just that — I wanted to *be* a mom. To do things differently. More than anything. I was tired of my life being at a standstill. I was tired of feeling like I was waiting for everyone else to do their part in order for me to move forward. So when you decided to go on tour this past spring, to move your life forward, I decided it was time to move mine."

Fuck. Julie played with her nails, unable to tear herself away from the look of shock — horror? — written on Anthony's features. She bit her lip and took a step closer.

He started to take a step back but stopped.

Whelp. She'd known that in this situation, the chances he'd leave were much higher than the ones where he stayed. She didn't blame him. If anything, Julie blamed herself.

"Anthony... I know I should've told you sooner. And I'm sorry. I — I just... I couldn't believe that this was real. Us. So I made it where I would be okay if you left." She opened her mouth to keep going but he raised a hand to stop her.

"Julie. Stop. Just stop."

Her mouth clamped shut, her body heating from his reaction. She didn't really know how this would go. She thought there'd be more yelling. His calmness was more unsettling than any shout or thorny word he could throw her way.

Those broad shoulders she'd leaned on so many times fell. He ran his hand through his hair, the movement pulling his unbuttoned coat open and his shirt up, exposing a sliver of skin. What she would give to not be here. To be undressing him and loving him in the other room, knowing that they wanted the same things.

At least there was one thing they agreed on.

"Anthony, I wanted — want — to marry you, too. But I didn't want to keep waiting for something that I didn't even know if you wanted or not."

Anthony snorted and shook his head. "Julie, we said forever. I don't know what more you wanted, but this... I have no words for this."

The number of times their conversations had ended with some form of them sharing their devotion to eternity was lost on Julie. But they never included that binding commitment, that piece of paper she didn't even know she wanted so badly until this past year. She knew she'd crossed a line by not telling him. If she'd let him in from the get-go, they wouldn't be here right now.

"I need time to gather my thoughts, and I have so many fucking questions I'll need you to answer." Anthony looked around the room, his lips set in a thin line. "But I think the biggest problem I'm having, aside from you keeping this from me, not even including me, is that you thought you could use a child to make yourself feel better about your life. And that you'd find a way to make yourself feel better about your life in case I left. I... I'm fucking speechless, Jules. I need to leave."

If looks could kill, the one he gave her broke her into a million pieces. Stomped her heart into the ground and lit the remains on fire. This was beyond disappointment. It was beyond betrayal. It lived on a battlefield where the war had ended, a muted battle lost among cries of the injured and ghosts of the dead.

Defeat.

Julie let him walk past her. He sidestepped to avoid brushing her with his arm. What she would give for just a taste, a moment, of, *it's okay. I'm here.*

With the slam of the front door, he was gone. She knew he'd come back, if only to get answers to his questions. But he wouldn't stay.

She'd fired the last shot, not knowing that when she pulled the trigger, the bullet would circle back and lodge itself in her heart.

Julie fell to her knees and bowed, letting the pain sink through her until sleep overtook despair.

28

Foster.

Kid.

Anthony had lived in a dream state since he walked around the room Julie had designed. Based on the wide range of activities and reading levels pasted on the books, he gathered she hadn't known the age of the child she hoped to have in her care.

Child.

He looked around his dad's apartment from the cocoon of the couch. In all honesty, he hadn't given much thought to kids. He used to think kids weren't for him, that he'd fuck them up. Who'd want an alcoholic for a father? But then he met Julie. His blonde beauty, with a heart of gold and walls so fortified they put Fort Knox to shame. His views changed from never ever, to only with her. And something way down the line. His three year plan had jumped from his tongue when facing her, but it had been a surprise even to him. He'd thought closer to five or ten. Maybe closer to ten.

But now?

Anthony sat up when he heard his apartment buzzer. Gideon was here, and he'd brought Ella, per Anthony's instructions. If anyone could help him sort through this mess, and bear the brunt of his anger and confusion, it'd be his cousin and Julie's best friend.

He buzzed his friends up and plopped back on the couch. Gideon had his own key and let himself and Ella in, not saying a word as they took off their winter attire. Anthony stared at the coffee table, imagining Julie, the love of his life, going behind his back with this.

"Hey, man." Gideon sat across from him while Ella sat beside him.

Ella avoided his gaze, shifting in her seat.

"You knew." The words left Anthony's lips, his gaze daring her to face him.

Gideon looked between the two. "What?" He stopped at Ella, who gave him a pleading look.

"I'm sorry! I couldn't break her trust." She

covered her face with her hands. "I didn't know what to do."

Gideon looked in disbelief at Anthony before turning back to his fiancée. "Are you kidding me, El? We're engaged, this is kind of something you share with me. How long have you known?"

Her face was flushed while she shook her head. "Not that long, I swear. She waited until after she'd made up her mind to do it to tell me and Rachel. But we kept telling her to tell you, Ant. I swear it."

"Rachel knows?"

"And Ben," Ella said.

Anthony couldn't believe his ears. This was the world's greatest prank, everyone but him knowing that his partner had applied to be a foster parent. He'd looked up the steps when he'd arrived home from her apartment. He knew it wasn't a small thing, but seeing the steps hit him. She'd gone to so much trouble to make it happen. And then she'd gone to so much trouble to keep it from him. And everyone around her had known the truth.

"Anthony, I'm sorry. I know you're going through a lot right now, but please don't take this out on me."

"Oh, I'm sorry if the love of my life hid the fact she was actively trying to bring a child into her life without even talking to me, her partner, about it. I'm sorry if she kept me completely in the dark and, lo and behold, you, her best friend, has all the deets."

"So what do you want from me, Anthony? I can't time travel and tell you or have her tell you sooner. It's done. So what do you want from me?" Ella had found her strength. Anthony had known she was feisty from Gideon, but he'd rarely been on the receiving end. That had always been Julie.

He stared at Ella, who looked so much like Julie they could be sisters. But he never felt the pull with Ella that he felt for Julie. The way Anthony saw Julie was the way Gideon looked at Ella. But that didn't mean their resemblance wasn't a harsh reminder of the woman who'd caused him so much pain.

"I don't know," he said. "I don't know how to move forward. Of all the ways that conversation could've gone, with all the hidden truths she could've laid out, fostering was not what I was expecting."

Gideon sighed. "Yeah... When you texted me I was thrown for a loop. I can't believe you kept that from me, El."

Ella hugged herself. "I'm sorry, babe. Can we talk about it when we get home? I think Anthony needs our help more right now."

Gideon nodded with the confidence that only a

loving, long-term relationship could bring. This was a hiccup in their relationship, not a dealbreaker. Anthony couldn't say the same about his and Julie's relationship.

"I don't know if I can get over her doing this," Anthony said. "She lied to me. Actively lied to me. She went behind my back. And okay, sure, we both should've brought up where we saw this relationship going. I'll take that one. But how do I get over the lying?"

"I think you need to decide what you want and what it's worth to you. Do you even want kids? To foster? Do you want that with Julie, knowing there are trust issues?"

"But haven't I done that to her?" Anthony looked up. His bout with rehab had been the first thing to impact their relationship. When he'd gotten out, she'd let him in and then turned him down. But she'd come back, and they'd moved forward. Until they'd stopped, somewhere between that new start and the ending he'd always dreamed for them.

"Ant, you cannot hold that over yourself." Ella's voice was stone. "Trust me, after the Ruby shit, Julie has moved so far from the rehab stint. She's taken you as you are. She has her limits, but that wasn't one of them."

"Will we always be leaving and coming back?"

"No, but you need to figure out at what point enough is enough." Gideon's voice was hushed, and he hazarded a glance at Ella. They'd made sacrifices and compromises to make it work, and here they were, engaged and ready for this next chapter.

Anthony wanted to see that with Julie, but he didn't know how a foster kid could possibly fit into his future.

29

"And you're sure it's okay for me to dip out this afternoon? I know I took time off last week, I hate to do it again." Julie looked at Rachel across the conference room table. It was a matter that should've been taken up with Priya in HR, but it was only a meeting.

Granted, a meeting with the foster agency, but still. It shouldn't take more than half a day.

Even though she had no idea what they wanted to meet about.

Rachel leaned back in the plush leather spinning chairs they'd bought for their conference room, her manicured hands folded over her stomach. Endlessly chic, her brown skin glowed against her cream blouse, the thin gold bracelets tinkling against each other on her wrists. Julie remembered learning during one of Rachel's family brunches that they had been a gift from Rachel's Nani when she'd visited one year from Pakistan.

"Of course not, Julie. As far as my deadlines, you're ahead of schedule. While I appreciate you making an effort to be in the office, you know I'm lax about that as long as the work gets finished." She smiled her pearly smile, teeth perfectly straight. "Everything okay?"

Did she mean with work? Anthony? The meeting?

Even Julie was having trouble keeping her shit straight.

The only thing that seemed to be okay was her family. While they were in touch about as often as before The Big Talk, there was no longer this invisible weight on Julie's shoulders.

"Jules?"

"Sorry, yeah. Yeah, everything's fine." She forced a smile, but by the expression on Rachel's face, it was obvious she didn't buy it.

"Okay. Well, you know I'm always here if you want to talk. Maybe we could do a Girl's Night next week?" For once, Julie could've sworn Rachel seemed desperate, but the questioning tone and puppy eyes quickly disappeared. Rachel was always flitting about town — that was why they could never do Girl's Nights anymore.

"Yeah, I'm sure we could work something out." Julie gave her friend, her boss, a small smile. "Thanks again for today, I really appreciate it."

"Of course." Rachel took her leave, her thick wavy hair swinging from her walk in five-inch stilettos as she entered the main office area. Ruby glanced up from her desk real quick before her pale cheeks turned beet red and her computer became the most interesting thing she'd ever seen. The other girls kept their heads down, doing their jobs. Julie checked her phone. She could kill two hours before leaving.

Their lawyers had filed for 501(c) status, which was the first major legal step to fulfilling Maven Media's — but mainly Julie's — nonprofit dreams. They'd follow up with filing for an Employer Identification Number in case they couldn't use Maven Media's, and she and Rachel would continue to work on drafting the bylaws. They'd already recruited who would be on the board to start. Once the bylaws were finished, they could host their first board meeting, set the accounting for the year, and start implementing their fundraising plan. Once it was settled what the various arms of Wings would do, the lawyers would figure out what business licenses and permits they needed to apply for.

By the time Julie had caught up on the 501 email, forwarded it to Rachel, Priya, and Leo, reviewed the bylaw draft, and added some of her mom's ideas to the fundraising document, her calendar dinged.

Her heart jumped up into her throat.

Stealing a quick glance at Rachel, who give a slight nod in return, Julie threw on her jacket and grabbed her purse. Moving her feet felt unnatural, the air around her buzzing as she made her way from the office in Brooklyn to the Manhattan agency in Tribeca. She didn't remember navigating the subways, only the way everything stopped moving once she reached the doors.

Tall windows stared at her, armed by their black iron frames. Julie swallowed the lump in her throat. She hadn't been to the space since after the initial orientation, handing over her identification documents, tax returns, medical history, and the like. Knowing how far she'd come, standing before her future now, Julie was overwhelmed. This was it.

She entered the building and gave her name to the receptionist. The chairs were comfortable, the walls white with inspiring posters and helpful phone numbers.

"Juliette Milligan?" The voice was strong, calm.

Julie raised her hand like she was in middle school, seeing the speaker was a tall woman, her braided hair beads reflecting the overhead lights. Julie stood, the woman shrinking several inches shorter than Julie. This was a woman who commanded a room.

"Hi Ms. Milligan, thanks for coming. I'm Jillian Buchanan." Ms. Buchanan's face broke out into a wide grin, her smile completely changing her face. As Ms Buchanan clasped her outstretched hand in greeting, Julie wanted nothing more than to sit with this woman and her warmth.

"Thanks so much for calling me. I'm excited but must also say a bit nervous." Julie couldn't stop the laughter that escaped, and she mentally kicked herself for showing just how nervous she was.

Ms. Buchanan chuckled as she led Julie to a small office in the back. "Oh honey, I get it. Trust me. Take a seat."

Julie did as she was told, taking in the butter-yellow walls adorned with a few pictures of Jillian and kids as well as a couple of degrees. Fake plants lined the single windowsill behind Jillian as she sat in front of her computer.

"So I think we have a placement for you. Your

home visit looked great, especially for an older child. However, my job is to ensure the safety of the child and to find the healthiest living situation for them." Jillian folded her hands on her desk, her eyes hard as she stared into Julie's soul. "We generally don't have issues with single foster parents or young foster parents, but there are points of concern. I understand you're single, which allows access for you to be dating and bringing strangers around the child. As I'm sure you can guess, this is not allowed unless we've met with the person. If a person were to live with you, they would first need to go through our application process and become certified. Along with that, because you are young, we — and especially I — worry about the age difference between a foster parent and their child. Sometimes the lines between friend and parent can be blurred by age. Given the nature of my work, it's imperative that a stable parental relationship comes first."

"Now, you've never been a parent. I know you've volunteered with children in the past, but raising a child is different than volunteering with one. We trust you understand these points of concerns and will notify me should anything change, correct?"

"Absolutely. I completely understand." Julie did everything in her power to keep her voice straight.

She clenched her purse in her lap, palms sweaty against the leather. Now that Anthony knew about her plans, she'd forgotten he would also have to become licensed. Eight weeks of training, medical records, everything. She nearly threw up at the thought of Jillian learning about his rehab and the way her dark eyes would ice over at the information.

That is, if he stayed.

"Great. So, with all that in mind, here's your child." Jillian's smile returned, the woman nearly bouncing out of her chair with excitement as she slid the file across the desk.

Julie held it in her hands, knowing this was one of those beautiful, scary moments when her life would forever be changed once she opened it.

There was no going back.

30

Anthony really tried to bring his A-game to band practice. And by the look on their label rep's face, they had all succeeded in doing so. Nate leaned against the wall behind Tom. Arms crossed, head bobbing to the beat. The band had had to sub some parts with pre-recordings, but if Nate approved, they could record it live.

When the band stopped and the pre-recording faded out, Nate pushed off the wall and gave a light clap.

"That was great, guys. Definitely a direction I didn't see coming, but I think it's a good one. Let's replace some of the heavy sax parts with guitar, to try and maintain some of those indie rock roots your fans love." He ran his hand through his short brown hair, turning nervously to Tom. Tom's slight nod filled Anthony with dread.

Nate turned back around, his smile more like a grimace.

"So I talked with Tom here about moving forward."

Anthony swore he could hear everyone's breathing in the quiet room.

"And I know we talked about the original schedule — record the album later this month and January, open for The Strokes February through May, take off June through August, hit the road with your own tour September to December."

Fuck.

"Now, I still think that's solid. But I talked with my bosses, and they want you doing festivals in the summer. Slowly drip those new singles in May and June, release the album in July, and BOOM! — " Nate clapped his hands, causing everyone to jump — "we're off like a rocket in August through December. Now, Tom said you guys would resist, but... contracts. My bosses are your bosses." Shrugging his shoulders, he looked around the room.

Where the fuck did he get off telling them how

long they'd be on the road for? Anthony felt his resolve slipping. Aside from him wanting time to rest and time away from the constant sober partying of his rock star life, the shit with Julie came barreling like a train to the front of his mind. He still didn't have an answer for how to move forward with her, but an extra three months on the road certainly wasn't going to help. Nate's face was looking rather punchable, and based on the way Gideon tensed and Ryan looked ready to pounce, he'd bet his life they felt the same. Only Max and Lucas looked defeated, staring at the ugly gray carpet under their feet.

"Look, I get it. Take time to adjust to the idea, I'll reach out to Tom later this week." Nate cleared his throat and gave a little wave before seeing himself out.

Anthony hoped the door would hit him.

It didn't.

Anthony turned to his bandmates, stewing in their anger. Everyone's eyes were on Tom, who hesitantly stood up from his seat behind the folding table.

"I know, I know. I'm reviewing the contracts again, see what loopholes there are to get out of it.

We have one year left in our contract, but with this next album we will have fulfilled our deliverable obligation of an EP and two albums." He looked at each of them, one by one. "Believe it or not, I have a life and would rather not be on the road for ten months next year."

"So what do we do?" Max's deep timbre almost always had a calming edge to it.

Even he was rattled.

Tom shrugged. "Honestly? I don't know. Right now, assume we can't get out of it. The contracts stipulate we work their schedule — with room for 'approval' — but at the end of the day, they pay us. They own us. I'm reviewing the language with lawyers, and also trying to see if... if we could break the contract."

"What?" Lucas looked like he was ready to flip the folding table.

A rush flew through Anthony's ears.

"B—Break the contract?" Had he heard correctly?

Tom sighed. "I'm out of options, guys. I wanted to review every course of action."

"4AD is literally one of the biggest music — not just rock — labels of all time." Gideon also sounded like he didn't believe what he'd heard. "So if we leave them, then what?"

"We go to a bigger label," Ryan said softly. "Or no label."

Leaving a label after three years wasn't uncommon, but the circumstances surrounding the departure mattered. No one wanted a fly-by-night client. Having the new album could work in their favor; they could shop it to the other big labels — Sony, Warner, Universal, EMI. But there was always the chance no one would pick them up.

Based on the silence that followed Ryan's statement, Anthony assumed everyone was thinking the same thing.

It was a gamble.

"I'm doing my best to not put us in that situation, but you guys need to decide if staying with the label is worth the changed tour schedule. And if we have to do festival season, we should also think on what we want to do once we are released from the contract. Because after the fall, they'll either hit us with a renewal or a release."

"This is such bullshit." Gideon set his guitar in its stand, stomping out of the room. The other guys watched him leave before ambling after him, leaving Anthony and his dad in the room.

"I'm sorry, Ant." Tom's mouth was set in a thin line, the disappointment written in his crow's feet.

He followed the rest of the band, leaving Anthony with his hands in his pockets, the weight of reality settling over him. If they were gone for the next year, he wasn't sure Julie would stay.

31

Can you come over?

Julie hesitated adding *We need to talk* to the text. That never went well.

She sent what she had, hoping Anthony wasn't in the middle of anything.

Now?

Yeah. Please.

Three dots. No dots. Three dots.

Give me an hour.

Julie bit her lip, unable to stop herself from shaking. An hour was a long time when your relationship was on the brink. Looking around her apartment, she thought of ways to occupy herself. She picked up a book from the coffee table. It took her a few minutes to realize she'd opened it upside down, and she promptly closed it. Reading was too much work. She'd cleaned the apartment this morning, in case Anthony was closer than an hour away.

Pacing. She'd just pace.

That lasted until Julie found herself outside of the child's bedroom. She'd started leaving the door open, now that the truth was out. The light streaming into the hallway reflected the lightness she'd felt telling Anthony. Finally. She knew keeping things to herself was a weight she didn't need. She knew it did more harm than good.

Maybe this time she'd learn.

Gazing around the room, she'd added more art supplies since reading the child's file. Apparently, seven-year-old Henry had an affinity for crafts. And had always wanted to learn guitar. Julie pictured his sweet little face, using the picture that had been in his file as a blueprint for all the moments she'd share with him. His mousy brown hair was long, his nose spattered with freckles, stars she couldn't wait to turn into constellations with every hug, every kiss. His glasses were a little too big, sliding down the bridge of his nose in the photo. Julie imagined Anthony teaching him guitar, those big glasses sliding as he worked his small fingers over the strings. His gap-toothed smile as he smiled at the love of her life. She couldn't begin to fathom what he'd been through at such a small age. She knew the details — the abuse, his mom in rehab for the sixth time, his dad in prison — but those words would never do justice to the scars they'd left on his skin, his mind, his dreams.

This had to work.

A knock on her door pulled her back to the white walls, the neat bed, the dusty guitar in the corner she may have to learn, in case Anthony decided this wasn't the life he wanted. That she had pushed him too far.

She opened the front door without a word, tried to avoid watching him peel off his coat, the fall of his hair when he took off his beanie. The pull of his shoulders against a waffle-knit henley, midnight blue. Sleeves pushed to three-quarters, baring his muscular forearms.

"I guess we should do this?"

His baritone voice called her eyes to meet his. They were frozen, steely, hardened to whatever information she might throw at him. Julie recoiled. She'd known what she'd done to him, but seeing it written in the way he looked at her, kept his distance from her, had her in pieces.

"Can I get you anything to drink?" The words

had been more hushed than she'd planned or wanted. So much for showing strength.

"Nah, but I want to have this conversation in the room. That room."

She tightened her sweater around her and led the way, holding onto each of his heavy footsteps as an anchor.

He had come. He was here. He hadn't left.
Yet.

They sat on the bed and turned to one another. Julie realized this was the first time it had been used in weeks. Depressions were already laid into the mattress and bedspread before Henry would arrive. She'd hoped he'd be the first to mark it. Not this conversation.

"Since you invited me over, maybe you should start." Anthony's voice had regained some strength, and Julie had to give him credit. He never let his gaze slip, didn't fidget with the cloth beneath them or tap a pattern on the floor. He was still.

Better to rip off the band-aid. "I met with the agency. They think they'll have a placement for me, in the next week or two. They're going over some of the legal stuff with the state Child Protection Agency, but Henry is a seven-year-old boy who like arts and crafts, has trouble reading, and wants to learn guitar. And he has freckles. And huge glasses." Julie caught herself smiling, remembering his picture. When Anthony didn't speak, didn't move, her smile dropped.

Of course she would be excited but he wouldn't be. She'd dropped an atomic bomb on him last time and had just rounded that out with another one. He was still probably getting used to the idea of the first one. If he had even decided to stay. Julie took a deep breath at the same time he did.

"4AD wants us to do the festival season. Tom's trying to find a way out of it, but he said he's not sure he'll be able to, and to plan on it."

Speaking of bombs.

Julie went over the math in her head, her eyes widening at the added tour time.

"Ten months?" she squeaked out.

"Ten months." His response was a whisper.

She cleared her throat. "Well, the agency said that any partner I bring around Henry would have to be approved. And any parent in the household would have to be licensed. But if you're on tour... I guess..."

She couldn't bring herself to say it.

"If I'm not here, that won't matter," he said.

How he found the words for her, she didn't think she'd ever understand.

"Anthony... I want you here. I know I fucked up. And I'm sorry. I think I've finally learned my lesson, but I beg that it's not at the price of losing you."

He met her with a sigh. "Even if we decided to stick together, with this tour I'll be gone for almost the first year of Henry being with you. I hadn't really given kids much of a thought, and now we're jumping into having a seven-year-old? I'd wanted to get married and spend time with you before kids entered the picture. And maybe we wouldn't be here if you'd just spoken to me. But we are here, and I don't know what to do with it. Because I love you, and I want to be with you, but I don't know how this could work with the way things stand."

"What are you saying?" The thump of Julie's heart overtook her senses; she barely made out his response.

"I think we need some time. I need to figure out the band stuff, and the fostering... thing. Julie... If we're going to do this, we need to do it all the way. Live together, get married, all of it. I'm tired of the in and out. But if I need to apply for the fostering license or whatever it is, how do you think they'll feel about alcoholism? If we want to make this work, it means putting both of our dreams on hold. I wouldn't be able to tour with the guys, and you wouldn't be able to have Henry while we sorted through the certification process."

"So it's either we put everything on hold in order to do it together, or we accept being separate in order to move forward?"

"Basically. I think. Jules, I just don't know, but that's what it sounds like, right?"

Thinking he'd be able to seamlessly, effortlessly merge with her plans had been stupid. So fucking stupid. Why she'd allowed herself those daydreams, for months… But she knew why. They'd helped her get through the long days of summer and cold nights of winter with Anthony away on tour. They'd helped Julie feel as though maybe, just maybe, she could have it all. After all they'd been through, she'd thought they'd be standing at the end of the road together.

"I'm not ready to make a decision."

His laugh was soft, his eyes glassy. "Me neither, sunshine. I love you, and we'll figure this out."

Anthony stood and took a look around the room. "It's a lovely space, Jules. Whoever ends up here is lucky."

Julie watched him leave, his words sinking like a

stone in her belly. She urged her feet to follow him. They reached the front door and Anthony turned around. Julie couldn't tear her gaze away from his feet. He'd worn his nice leather oxfords, the top of his black jeans hiding the laces. She didn't want him to leave, but didn't know how to get him to stay.

Finally meeting his eyes, Julie took a sharp breath. The sadness rolled off him in waves. It hit her, consumed her, moving its way over and through her, pulling her closer to him. Cautiously, carefully, she reached a hand to his chest. She closed the distance between them, if only for a moment. He held her gaze before wrapping her in his arms. This wasn't a usual hug. It wasn't filled with passion or lust. There were no stray hands finding skin under shirts or back pockets begging for a squeeze. This was hollow. Heavy. It held until Julie felt like they were melding into one. This felt like goodbye.

32

Anthony looked around the living room, trying to not remember the last time the band had gathered in his home. Trying not to remember the amber liquid Tom nonchalantly brought, despite three members of the band being sober. Trying not to remember how, in his moment of human weakness, he went searching for it. He told himself it wasn't to drink but rather to know if his dad would leave a vice lying around. What he'd found was the proof of an affair, a nail in the coffin of his parents' marriage. This time, Tom hadn't brought anything more than chips and soda, the brightly colored bags and cans staring at Anthony. Mocking him.

He wasn't sure how to feel about the missing drink.

"Thanks for coming guys." Tom cleared his throat. Anthony noticed his silver hair returning to its original black in the low light and realized how much his dad had aged over the last few years.

"What's the deal with the contract, Tom?" Ryan wasted no time.

"Well, good and bad news. What do you want first?"

Anthony almost laughed at the overwhelming unison that asked for the bad news first. Sometimes his life felt crazy, and dealing with a record label could only make it crazier.

"We have to finish the album. They'll continue to own all the rights to your music, but based on what the lawyers said, once we fill our contractual obligations, we can leave. Touring wasn't an obligation, and because of your almost overnight success, this album will finish out the contract and your advance."

"But then for the fall we won't be headlining a tour," Lucas said.

"Yeah. Basically, there's a few options. One, we do what they want this year and bail next year. Two, we push back on the festival tour. With our contract entering renegotiations next year, there's a chance they'll want to keep us happy. Three, we finish the album and bail in February or March, but armed with another album to shop to a new label. I worry not having that next label will put you in the *irrelevant* category."

Gideon shrugged. "Seems obvious to me."

"What if pushing back on festival season doesn't work?" Max shook his head, rubbing his sparse beard. "We should have another plan of action."

The guys looked at one another.

Anthony thought of Julie, the life he wanted to lead with her. The ways he'd be able to contribute and support. He met Gideon's eyes, knowing his cousin was thinking the same thing about Ella. Gideon nodded, giving Anthony the go-ahead.

"I don't think three's an option. If we want to keep doing this — which I know we all do — we can't risk irrelevancy. We have to push back on festival season and hope they want to keep us happy enough to let it slide. Otherwise, let's all gear up for touring for ten months next year." Anthony scoffed. Saying it out loud highlighted how ridiculous it was for 4AD to expect — and pay for — the indie rock band Eternal Youths to travel for a whole year. It's not like they were The Rolling Stones.

"We should probably figure out if we want to

stay with them. You know, if we're talking about moving forward anyway." Ryan looked around the room.

"You're not wrong. For me, it depends on how they handle this tour thing. They've been good to us — they put us on the map, they got us Imagine Dragons and The Strokes." Max shook his head. "Hell, we'll be earning royalties after this album release. Everything from our headlining tour will be split fifty-fifty with them. We're young to be in this position."

"I agree," Lucas and Gideon said at the same time.

"Personally... I don't want to stay with them," Ryan said. "I'm tired of touring. They keep pushing and pushing and I'd like to have, you know, a year off? Actually work on an album that's good." Ryan's voice was rising, his frustration apparent in the red flush on his fair skin, showing even under his crew cut blond hair.

"Actually? What's that supposed to mean? I think our albums are pretty fucking awesome." Max never swore, and he never threw daggers. But his eyes were telling a different story, grilling Ryan until he looked away.

"Not as in, you know, *actually* good. As in *actually*

taking the time to explore the music we create before putting it out. I just want more time."

"K, just checking."

Anthony pursed his lips, cutting the tension with a low whistle. "Damn, boys. Why don't we just wait to see what they say about the tour before going at each other?"

"You have no room to talk, Russo." The anger had reappeared in Ryan's voice. Anthony felt chided at the reminder of the shit he'd pulled before, the drunken mess he and Gideon had both been. The fight between him and Tom. Ryan might have a point, but they were a group. If one person was off, it affected everyone. He held up both hands, a point of surrender.

"I'm just saying, it's too early to figure it out. Something to think on, sure, but no need to get our panties in a twist."

Ryan opened his mouth, but Tom cut him off. "We all need to chill. I'll talk to Nate, see what he says. Everyone's been heard. I thought tonight we could hang out like we used to, get some pizza or Mexican and watch a movie."

"Sounds good to me, hoss." Max shrugged, grabbing a bag of chips and plopping on the sofa. Gideon followed with a different bag and a box of Cokes.

The tension slowly dissipated, the rest of the guys settling in and joking around while they flipped through the streaming platforms. Tom was trying to get everyone's thoughts on food. Anthony glanced at Ryan, arms crossed, jaw clenched. His bandmate was staring at the screen, but Anthony knew he wasn't paying attention.

Given his attitude and the things he'd said, maybe Ryan didn't want out from just the label.

33

She knew she needed to tell Jillian about Anthony — even as a heads up maybe — but as Julie stood in the park waiting to meet Henry for their first visit, she didn't think she'd have the heart to. Telling Jillian would create all sorts of hiccups, and could ruin Julie's chances at this. Especially if he decided it wasn't for him, she would've told Jillian for nothing.

Julie bounced on the balls of her feet. She'd bought new Keds for the occasion so they'd look fresh, clean, like she could take care of a seven-year-old if she could take care of herself. Her jeans were a bit tighter than she'd expected, the old faithful pair having been around for years. Perfectly stretched, perfectly soft. The December wind bit at her exposed ears, her gray scarf the only thing keeping her neck from freezing. She'd put her hair in a ponytail, in case Henry wanted to run around or play on the playground.

"Juliette!" Jillian's voice called down the walk, her gloved hand raised in a wave. Her hair beads were gone, her hair left to its natural state, bouncing with every step. Her smile was measured but toothy, betraying some of the excitement she must've felt. It must've felt good to place a child with a loving parent.

In her other hand, she led a small boy. His jeans slightly falling, his finger pushing those oversized glasses up his nose. He shuffled, keeping his eyes to the ground. Behind him strode a young woman with a straight bob, severe in the way it framed her angular face. No smile and a clipboard in her arms. A man deep in middle age followed her, briefcase in hand. He gave Julie a small smile when they reached her.

"Jillian." Julie couldn't stop herself from beaming as she shook her hand. "Hi, I'm Julie. You must be the CPS workers." She extended her hand to the angular woman, the graying man.

"Hi, I'm Eric and this is Cara. We're Henry's caseworkers." His voice was pleasant, while Cara kept studying Julie. She felt as though she were under a microscope, a specimen that would never pass whatever rigorous mandates Cara instilled. Julie swallowed before kneeling before the little boy.

"And you must be Henry. It's nice to finally meet you." Julie remembered her volunteering day in India, where the atmosphere was full of calm, trust, and friends. She kept her voice soft, her smile gentle. "Can I give you a hug?"

Henry swung Jillian's hand and nodded. Wrapping her arms around his skinny frame, Julie breathed in the earthy scent of his hair. Warm, like grass on a summer day. He snaked his arms around her briefly before letting go and returning his hand to Jillian's.

Julie stood and turned to Jillian. "I'm so glad we could do this, thanks for reaching out."

"My pleasure. It's a mandate we have two public visits with CPS present before we do the first overnight. We figured we could sit on the bench across from you while you two get to know each other, maybe go for a short walk, given the cold?"

"Perfect." Julie huddled against the wind while Jillian explained to Henry. Cara looked over her shoulder as she moved with the others to the opposite bench. Once they sat, she didn't take her eyes off Julie.

Julie sat next to Henry on the bench, listening to the shrieks of kids on the playground behind her. Henry swung his legs, picking at a loose thread on his coat. She let the silence sit, let him warm up to her presence. She looked down at him, quiet and sad.

"It's so cold today." Weather was always a good starting place.

He nodded.

Julie looked around. Breaking the wall was always the hardest part. Cara still stared her down, but Eric and Jillian were laughing loud and frequently. Julie smiled.

"What makes you laugh, Henry?"

He bit his lip and pushed his glasses up. When he turned to her, his big brown eyes were earnest.

"Jokes."

"Jokes? Well, Henry, I'm the *queen* of jokes. I'm always looking for more. Do you have any? I bet you're funny."

He scrunched his mouth, deep in thought.

"What did the left eye say to the right eye?"

Julie pretended to think, not wanting to give

away that this was a favorite among the kids in India. "I really don't know. What?"

"Between us, something smells!" Henry's smile lit a fire in her heart. Gap-toothed and wide, it didn't need a laugh for her to know just how funny he thought that was. She gave him a loud laugh instead.

"That's a good one! Why did the kid eat his homework?"

Henry looked to the sky. "I don't know, why?"

"Because his teacher told him it was a piece of cake!"

That brought a giggle to his lips, and Julie relished in the sweet sound.

They spent the remainder of their afternoon trading jokes before the lowering sun and cruel wind pulled Jillian, Eric, and Cara back over to them. Julie hated that their time had come to an end, but judging by the look on Jillian's and Eric's faces, there'd be a next time.

"Sounded like you were having a lot of fun, Henry!" Jillian ruffled his long hair, setting her hand on his shoulder.

He smiled up at her. "We told lots of jokes."

"That's good. I like jokes, maybe you can tell me some after I speak with Julie for a moment?" She gave him a nudge toward Cara and Eric while Jillian pulled Julie for a short walk.

"I swear, child, I haven't seen him laugh like that in ages. Thank you."

The heat spread through Julie's body. "Thank *you*, Jillian. He's such a sweetheart."

"He is, isn't he? Such a bright light despite all the darkness he was brought up in. I'm glad you had a great time." Jillian stopped and turned to Julie. "Think on everything, and please let me know any changes or concerns you may have. I'd like to schedule a second visit for next week and a house sleepover the following week. We're keeping our options open and want to find the best fit for him."

Julie crossed her arms against the cold. She knew this was the process, but it still hurt knowing it wasn't a done deal. That she wasn't the unquestionably best choice. But Jillian was doing her job — making sure Henry found the best fit for him. It was nothing personal, something Julie needed to remind herself. "I completely understand. Give me a call and we'll figure out another meeting. I'd love to see him again."

The furrow between Jillian's brow released, a smile blooming between her cheeks. "Wonderful. Have a great rest of your day, Julie." She gave a small pat on Julie's arm before turning back to the CPS workers, Eric laughing at something Henry said and Cara marking something on her clipboard.

Julie watched them walk away, gripped with the need to follow. This was everything she'd truly wanted, even if it'd taken her years to figure it out.

34

Anthony noticed the tension in Ryan's fingers as he plucked his bass strings. His blond bandmate had been quiet on the subject of touring, on renegotiating with 4AD, since the meeting at the apartment. The surliness infiltrated the room, the rest of the band low-energy.

"Guys, stop." Tom threw his hands up in exasperation. "Since you all seem to be in a bad mood, maybe we should focus on the ballads today."

Grumbling wound its way through the room. Ryan set down his bass and left, Lucas climbing out from behind the drums to follow him. He called out they were going to hang out in the building's communal space for a bit before he disappeared.

Max took a seat next to Tom at the folding table. The two men stared at Gideon and Anthony.

"What?" Gideon looked around. "I don't have anything ready."

"I thought you said you were working on something?" Anthony met his cousin's stare.

"Yeah, your stuff. Do you have anymore?"

"What do you think's on the table?" Anthony nodded to the folder in front of Tom.

"No need to be a dick." Gideon strutted to the table, flipping the black folder open and pulling out sheets of paper. Anthony saw his barely legible scrawl as Gideon flipped through the pages. Max's laugh rang out.

"Dude, we need a cipher or somethin' to read that chicken scratch."

"Beggars can't be choosers. I have a couple things but they need work."

Tom cleared his throat. "Ant, you got any that would work with the sax?"

Anthony made his way to Gideon and pulled the sheets from his cousin's hands. He sorted the pages on the table in piles, one for piano, one for guitar, and one that could incorporate the full band. The way Max played sax was how Anthony imagined old jazz clubs, notes ringing through a haze of smoke, weaving their way between bodies pressed together but not close enough. Where love and lust and loss knew their home. He bit his lower lip, pulling the sheets from Gideon's hands. The space Max occupied was a hard one to reach, but there was one piano ballad that could work. He found it and brought the sheet over to the keyboard, setting his hands up.

Anthony closed his eyes, remembering the night he and Julie stood before the Washington Square arch. The night they'd almost kissed, when being near her hurt more than not being with her. He'd wanted to wrap his arms around her, pull her into him in a dance beneath the stars. His fingers trailed along the keys, the opening notes soft, almost hopeful, before pausing and launching into a repeat. He wasn't the singer, not since before his accident. He'd become tone-deaf, and no doctor had been able to restore the skill. So he hummed the lyrics he'd written. Lyrics that sung of love and loss and letting go. Behind closed eyes he watched his relationship with Julie unfold. The fun, the hurt, the anger, the love. The unknown. The possibilities. He played through the song, finishing softly.

He blinked back tears and cleared his throat. "So, uh, yeah. I was thinking maybe on this part — " he replayed the chorus, humming along, " — Max could come in. Honestly, man, you can just feel it out. I trust you."

Max nodded, running his hands through his hair like he'd done when he'd had his dreads. "Yeah, that sounds good. What about on the part where you go —" he hummed the bit, and Anthony played the corresponding part on the keys, "— Yeah, that part. What if I add a little something there as well?"

"Great." Anthony looked up at his dad and Gideon. "What do you guys think?"

Tom nodded. "Yeah, that sounds great. Gideon, can you and Anthony go over the lyrics and key?"

"Sure." Gideon went to his cousin, and they reviewed the lyrics. Anthony hummed and played along while Gideon found his vocal stride. Max had picked up his sax, the notes sliding between sad and sultry.

Anthony wasn't sure how much time had passed before the other guys came back, but when Ryan walked through the door, he seemed calmer. His lower jaw was still set in a hard line, but his complexion had paled a bit. Lucas threw Tom a small smile, and Anthony caught his dad release a sigh.

"What do you guys have?" Lucas sat at the table, slouching down and crossing his arms.

Max flew into a riff on his sax, mixing the sound he'd just created with an old, famous pop song. The guys laughed, the tension easing even more.

"Nah, seriously though." Gideon looked at Max and Anthony. "Rough cut?"

Anthony nodded, taking his stance behind the keys and closing his eyes. Gideon counted off.

The first part of the song held Anthony's notes, haunting in the quiet room. But Gideon's deep baritone voice drew the ghosts from the ground, bringing life to them as the song dove into the chorus. Max's sax gave them movement, and Anthony could practically feel Julie pressed against him, her sad smile turning into a gentle kiss upon his cheek. While being a tortured artist certainly had its drawbacks, it was moments like this — when pain turned into beauty — that almost made the agony worth it.

Almost.

Gideon sang Anthony's lyrics, and Anthony was hit with just how much he and Julie had hurt each other. How much he'd hurt himself. How, if they continued together, they would continue to hurt one another.

How many more moments did they have where they could turn that pain into beauty?

35

Julie rose from the office desk, stretching in the glow of the street light outside. Working from home had its perks, but sitting for long stretches with no social breaks wasn't always one of them.

It'd been awhile since she'd cleaned, a fact she was reminded of as she made her way to the kitchen to figure out a dinner plan. She opened the fridge door and pursed her lips. The light from the fridge was even more stark in its emptiness. Maybe it'd be another takeout night.

The apartment intercom buzzed, making her jump. She checked her phone. Too late for any deliveries. No texts or missed calls.

Cautiously making her way to the box, she pressed the talk button.

"H-Hello?"

"Hi, Julie. We wanted to stop in for a surprise visit. Just to make sure everything was kosher." Jillian's voice made Julie's blood run cold.

Fuck.

"Oh! Oh sure thing, come on up." She pressed the buzzer and frantically looked around.

Jillian had said "we" — so Cara and Eric were probably tagging along. It'd take them a matter of minutes to reach her apartment. She looked around, wiping the counters and clearing work papers off the dining room table. Julie put the papers in the office and did one last sweep of Henry's would-be room, the mirror spurring her into Speed Racer.

Another downside to working from home: being in pajamas and having unexpected guests.

Julie ran to her room, clasping a bra on just as the knock sounded at her door.

"One minute!" She adjusted her shirt as she made her way to the door, thankful her pajama pants today were yoga leggings and not her ripped-up polka-dot capris.

Jillian gave her a smile, hands folded in front of her. Cara and Eric stood behind her, Cara as stiff as ever with her clipboard and Eric rocking back and forth on his heels.

"Sorry about that, I wasn't expecting anyone and was working from home today." Julie laughed nervously. "Can I get you guys anything to drink? Water, tea?"

"Well, that is the point of a surprise visit," Cara said. "A scheduled visit means applicants can prepare. A surprise means we arrive when things are in a state of normalcy." She wrote something on her clipboard, her heels clipping as she wandered around the kitchen.

"We're good, thanks for offering," Jillian said. "Just take a seat, we won't be more than a few minutes and then we can discuss a home visit for Henry." She looked around the space before trailing Cara, Eric bringing up the rear.

Sweat trickled down Julie's spine as she sat at the dining room table. They were silent as they judged her space, peering behind shelves and wandering down the hall. Their voices were murmurs that floated from the other rooms. The creak of old wooden doors and the click of sharp heels followed them back into the main living space. They passed her to check out her bedroom off the kitchen, Eric's face resting in a small smile and Jillian's more obvious.

Cara and Eric disappeared behind the door, but

Jillian froze in front of the dresser.

Two pictures stared back at her.

Julie's breath hitched. She'd left evidence of Anthony — a relationship with Anthony — in her bedroom, and Jillian had found it. Jillian turned, staring at Julie. No anger in her crow's feet or smile lines. Just disappointment. She disappeared behind the door to join Cara and Eric, their voices low.

The kitchen started to close in on Julie, a rushing invading her ears. Black spots dotted the white counters, the tiled backsplash. Julie gripped the table, closing her eyes to the waves. Without Jillian saying a word, she knew how this would end.

"Julie? Are you okay?"

She opened her eyes to Jillian's concerned face peering at her, a warm hand resting on her shoulder. Julie took a shaky breath.

"Y—Yeah, I'm good."

"Okay. We made some notes we'd like to go over with you."

The three took a seat on the large couch while Julie rose on shaky legs. She was almost unaware of how her feet took her to the armchair beside the couch, almost unaware of how her body lowered itself onto the cushions. The one thing she'd been careful to avoid was happening, and she didn't know how to stop it.

"So the living space looks great. It's clean, it's bright. The child's room has accounted for a myriad of activities." Jillian sighed. "Honestly, Julie, it's one of the better setups we've seen."

"But you failed to disclose a potential partner and parent for the child." Cara's voice was cold, her eyes trained on the clipboard in her lap.

Eric threw her a sympathetic smile. "Of course, it's not too late to add someone to the application, but they will need to give their consent to a background check."

"And unfortunately, the time it will take to clear a second person now puts your ability to foster on hold." Jillian cleared her throat. "But first things first — we need information on your relationship. How available will he be while you foster? How often does he reside in this apartment? What's his employment situation? Is he aware that you've applied for this?"

Julie looked her jury in the eyes. "He is aware of my decision. We've been together for a few years now. He works in the music industry, and he's on tour a fair amount."

"Why didn't you tell us sooner?" Eric's voice was soft, comforting. Fatherly.

"I— I wasn't sure what to say, to be honest. This is my thing, and I'm not sure if it's something he wants. So I was waiting to sort that out before having him submit an application."

"Don't you think you should've sorted that out before applying?" Cara's icy voice translated into her stare. Julie swallowed and glanced away.

"In hindsight, yeah. Probably. But I'm doing my best, as any parent would, and I don't want to waste anyone's time. I know what I want and I've never let someone stop me from getting it."

Jillian sighed. "Well, I can't say this doesn't cause some issues. If your partner submits his application in the next few days, we might be able to make it work for Henry. Provided he's cleared. But if he doesn't, and he isn't, then your application will be placed on hold while we sort this out. Is that clear?"

"Crystal."

"Okay then." Jillian rose, letting the other two leave first. When they'd gone through the front door, Jillian turned to Julie and placed a hand on her shoulder.

"I'm sorry this happened. To be honest, I think it's safe to say the timeline is too tight and Henry will not be placed in your care. I want you to set your own expectations and, going forward, I need you to be transparent with me. Otherwise this won't work. Take care, Ms. Milligan."

Julie was left standing in her doorway. She never let someone stop her from getting what she wanted.

Except herself.

36

Gideon shot the cue ball into the red solid, the red spinning across the table before dropping into the nearest pocket. Anthony high-fived his pool partner and walked around the table to give him room for another shot. Lucas rolled his eyes while Max shook his head. They never gave up facing Gideon, even though Anthony knew his cousin was good enough to compete.

The bar was relatively quiet for a Thursday night and had become a go-to when Anthony needed to get out of the house but didn't want to be tempted by the press of people and the sour alcohol odor that hung in the air. If the guys were here, he could be distracted enough to not think about it.

Coming alone was a different story.

Gideon dropped the ball he'd aimed for and moved to find a third score.

"Ah fuck. That sucks." Gideon shook his head at the missed shot, moving aside for Max to take a turn.

"How's Ella, Gid?" Anthony asked, cradling his cold seltzer. He knew Gideon liked these pool nights to hang with the guys, but he also knew Gideon missed Ella whenever they were apart.

"She's good, stressing about wedding stuff. Especially with the potential festival tour. We have a Plan B in case we need to do a small thing sooner rather than later. How's Julie?"

"No idea. We haven't spoken since that night." Anthony's heart hurt as the words tumbled out.

Gideon froze. "At all?"

"K, you're up Ant." Max shook his head and stepped aside.

Anthony looked at the table, noticing a missing stripe and a scratched cue ball. He got into position and answered Gideon.

"At all. I don't really know what to say." He sunk his target. "I want her. But there are clearly trust issues. And kids…" He sunk his second target, with groans coming from Max and Lucas behind him.

Missing his third target, Anthony turned to Gideon. He hesitated before saying the truth he'd always known, the one that had kept him from talking to Julie about their future in the first place. "I dunno. What if I'm a bad parent? What if I'm a bad partner?"

Gideon's shoulders relaxed as he looked at Anthony. Lucas called for Gideon's turn. "One minute, man," Gideon called out before lowering his voice. "Ant, I know it's been rough. I know your dad was gone a lot when you were younger, and I know your mom dropping off hurt. But I also know that you did whatever it took to be with Julie. That you did whatever you could to reach your mom. That you healed your relationship with your dad. That you continue to hold on when everything is telling you to let go. Sure, you've made mistakes. But what if you started forgiving yourself and letting all that shit go? What if you told her your fears and really let her in?"

"Hey guys, you okay?" Max came up next to Gideon, Lucas close behind.

Anthony nodded, Gideon's words racing through his head.

"Julie?" Lucas asked, looking between Gideon and Anthony.

"Yeah," Anthony muttered, pushing past them to shoot his turn. His mind spun. As much as he and

Julie had loved each other, they'd hurt each other. But that was every relationship he'd been in — with his parents, with Gideon, with himself. Subconsciously, he'd always felt Julie was different. Untouchable. Like he'd never amount to what she needed, or wanted, despite her saying otherwise. So he'd pushed her away. But he'd pushed so far that he played into her own fears, and she'd pushed back.

They kept forgiving and coming back to one another, and now they were at a breaking point. Anthony needed to figure out if he could accept his own flaws so they wouldn't stand between him and the only woman he'd ever loved, and the life he was beginning to feel he was meant for.

37

Ella stepped out of the dressing room and Julie couldn't stop the tears from welling. Her best friend was draped in creamy lace, the long sleeves of her wedding dress leading to a crew neck that highlighted her slender neck. The fabric clung to her torso, sheer over her arms and collarbone but lined along the bodice. It fell into a thick satin skirt that hugged her curves before flaring at the bottom. Ella's face was radiant, the front of the dress gathered in her hands as she turned and looked over her shoulder. While the lace in front had reached her neck, it plunged into a backless design with a few tiny buttons along her hips and butt.

"Oh, El." Julie was speechless. The look was old-fashioned with a modern twist, and she truly didn't believe she'd seen anything so beautiful.

Her best friend turned back to the mirror as Rachel exclaimed over the design. Ella bit her lip and met Julie's eyes in the mirror. "Do you like it?"

"Ella, it's stunning." Rachel stood, smoothing her black cigarette trouser pants as she walked over to Ella, bracelets tinkling as she fixed some of the bunched fabric in the back. The attendant stood off to the side, giving the girls their moment to enjoy just how far they'd come.

"I love this little detailing in the back." Rachel's thin fingers skimmed the buttons.

"Seriously, El. It's gorgeous. You're gorgeous." Julie wiped her eyes before joining her friends by the mirrors. She watched the engagement ring flicker in the light as Ella ran her hands over the smooth skirt.

Julie had always known her best friend would be the first of them to get married. Ever the hopeless romantic, Ella had kept herself at bay for so long her walls were bound to break. And they had, when she met Gideon. Julie had helped her friend's fiancé find the ring, a strained day but one that had given her hope that maybe — just maybe — she'd find someone worth breaking her walls for.

The attendant stepped forward to speak with Ella as Julie's phone vibrated in her pocket. Jillian's name flashed onscreen, Julie's heart jumping into her throat. With all the wedding planning, she hadn't had a chance to tell Ella or Rachel about the drop-in the other night.

Correction: she hadn't wanted to tell them.

"Sorry guys, I need to take this." She stepped away before they could answer.

"Hey, Jillian."

"Julie, hi. Thanks for answering."

"Of course. What can I do for you?"

"Well, we haven't received anything from your partner, and Henry's case is moving fast. We've decided to place him in another home."

Julie's heart dropped. She knew this would be the case, but hearing the words still stung.

"Are you there?"

"Sorry, yeah," Julie managed to say.

"One more thing. We've decided to place your application on hold for the time being. Given the lack of forthcomingness and the potential addition of a second parent, your situation reads as unstable for a foster child." Jillian paused, giving Julie time to make sure she'd heard her right. "I'm really sorry, Julie. Truly. Once you get those things sorted, please give me a call. I do think you'd be a wonderful fit for this, just not right now. Take care of yourself." Her voice had softened before she dropped the call, but the barbs were still there. They were lodged in Julie's lungs, her heart, her breath scrambling to find a way in and out.

Not right now.

Her whole life, people had kept leaving. Hannah, her friends, her parents. Herself. She'd done everything she could to steel herself against the possibility that it would keep happening. That she could be the one who stayed. But she'd been so terrified of losing this opportunity, of losing Anthony, that she'd done everything she wasn't supposed to, and now it was here to haunt her.

"Julie?" Rachel came to Julie's side while the boutique shop swam before her. Creams and golds bled with pastel pinks and deep reds.

"I — I need to sit down."

"Okay, okay. Here." Rachel's hand was firm on Julie's elbow as she led her to one of the tufted chairs scattered about. Rachel asked someone for water, the words muffled as the world started falling apart. Julie placed her head in her hands. This was a numbness, a grief, that couldn't bear the fruit of tears. All she could do was sit and allow herself to hum with the words she'd known all along but had refused to acknowledge.

"Babe, what happened?" Rachel knelt before Julie, a hand on her knee.

"Jillian found out about Anthony and they're putting my application on hold. She said my situation was too unstable. I knew I couldn't do this." Her voice cracked. "I knew I was making a mistake by not telling them but I couldn't tell Anthony and now I don't get anything. I don't get to foster and I've probably already lost Anthony and it's all just so stupid and I'm stupid. Why did I think this would work out?"

Rachel sighed. "Jules. Look, I'm not a therapist. But I do know you did what you thought was best. Anthony was in and out. You didn't have control over that. So you found control somewhere else. But you want to know the secret? You were never actually in control of anything. You never are. But we find things that give us a sense of control, and we hold on for dear life. You clung so hard to this, it broke. And that's okay. Do you know what you do have control over?" Rachel leaned forward. "How you move forward. I haven't left you. Ella hasn't left you. And you want to know who else hasn't left you?"

Julie heard the smile in Rachel's voice and

couldn't stop the tug at her own lips, thinking about the funny, complicated, sexy man she would always be in love with.

She shook her head. "He hasn't. *Yet.*"

"Oh, Julie. Why are you borrowing trouble? He hasn't left. There's no *yet* to play with, because it hasn't happened. I want you to say it until you believe it: *he hasn't left.*"

Julie sniffled, the words a loop in her head. *He hasn't left he hasn't left he hasn't left.*

Maybe Rachel was right. Maybe if she repeated them, eventually she'd believe them.

"Oh my god, Jules, are you okay?" Ella fell to the floor beside her, pushing Julie's hair away to look at her face. She was back in her street clothes. Julie nodded while Rachel filled her in.

"Oh, honey. I'm so sorry." Ella stood, her arms pulling Julie into a warm hug. "I know you were really set on this, but it hasn't gone anywhere. You're becoming the person you need to be, and when it's the right time, you can always call Jillian."

Julie stared at the sparkling diamond on her friend's finger. Somehow, with all the times she'd pushed and pulled, tested boundaries and drawn her own, there were people that stayed.

He hasn't left.

38

Tom held the door to the coffee shop open, letting Anthony walk through first. He ducked a couple exiting. This coffee shop was becoming a band favorite, the location prime but the space rarely bustling. The rest of the guys had asked to hold the next band meeting there for a change of scenery.

Anthony spied them in a back corner, Lucas's sunglasses dully reflecting the scene around them and Max's fedora pulled low. Ryan sat with his arms crossed, sulking. One of the blessings of being a musician was people rarely recognized you — they knew your music, not your face. But the more they toured, the more radio spots they got, the less that would be the case. Anthony threw the crew a quick nod before heading to the counter with his dad to grab coffees for the table. The barista was giggly, her eyelashes batted and her smile sweet. Anthony turned away as quickly as he could without seeming rude. He'd never be able to look at another woman without thinking of Julie.

He sat at the table while Tom placed the coffees in the center. They knew everyone's orders — the super sweet cappuccino for Max, the salted caramel soy latte for Ryan, the extra-chocolate peppermint mocha for Lucas, the small black coffee for Gideon — and Anthony took his own latte away from the mix. Tom sat beside him, sipping a rooibos tea. He waited for everyone to grab their drinks before clearing his throat.

"So, I have word from Nate and 4AD."

The table stilled, their future hanging in the silence.

"They're fine with us skipping festival season and doing our own headlining tour in the fall, but since we've met the terms of the initial contract prior to the termination date, we need to re-sign."

Anthony's shoulders relaxed, and he caught Gideon's eye. His cousin was beaming — he and Ella could have the wedding of their dreams that summer. Lucas and Max high-fived, their chatter with Tom over what new contractual terms they could ask for masking the sullenness wafting from Ryan's spot beside Anthony.

Anthony nudged his bandmate. "Dude, what's up? This is the outcome we all wanted."

Ryan shook his head, releasing a sigh. "Hey, guys?"

"What's up, man?" Max couldn't stop his smile from spreading.

"I need to talk to you." Ryan took a shaky breath. "I'm... I'm done. I want out."

It felt like someone had sucked all the air out of the room. His attitude the last couple of months finally made sense. But on the heels of the upcoming tour season...

"How long have you felt this way?" Tom's stern voice reached across the table, no room for negotiation.

"Um... Awhile, but I wanted to make sure before I said anything."

"You wanted to set yourself up before bailing?" Lucas's voice was venom. He and Ryan were almost as close as Anthony and Gideon. Anthony took a deep breath; if Lucas hadn't even known, Ryan really wasn't on their team anymore. He'd been out far longer than he was admitting.

"That's not it, man."

"Then what is *it*, Ry?" Max's voice was laced with disappointment. "You wait until we get the tour thing situated and then it's all, *'Oh, hey, y'all need a new bassist for your tour with The Strokes and the fall headliner!'* I thought you wanted to headline our own show?"

Ryan shrugged. "I do. Just..."

"Not with us." Anthony stared at his coffee, the words stinging as he said them. He should've been used to this, to people not wanting him.

"Yeah. I'm sorry, guys. Really. But this isn't the band I want to be in. It's not the music I listen to, it's not the vibe I want, it's just... not right. For me."

"For you." Lucas spat out his ex-best friend's words.

Anthony glanced at the two, Lucas's jaw clenched, his fair skin turning a red Anthony had never seen on his bandmate. Ryan shifted in his seat, avoiding the hard stares from all around.

"Did you get an offer?" Tom asked, a note of resignation in the way the words came out, in the way he sipped his tea.

It was the question playing at Anthony's mind, but the one he couldn't bring himself to ask.

"Y—Yeah. It's a newish band, called Stamped. They play what we used to. I just think it's a better fit." Ryan shifted in his seat and looked around the shop.

"I'm sorry, do you not want to be here?" Gideon snorted. "This is some fucking bullshit."

"This wasn't an easy call for me to make."

"Well, you sure didn't have any trouble holding it in until the last minute. No discussion, no warning, no nothing. It's like your foot's been halfway out the door this whole time."

"Gid, that's not true. I was there through it all. College, band practices, your issues, Anthony's shit. I'm glad you guys are happy with the way things turned out but I'm not. It's not a good fit anymore."

"I think," Tom interrupted, Gideon's mouth closing before he could fire another retort, "I think we all just wanted there to be more communication. To be honest, this really fucks things up, Ryan. I don't know how we'll get a bassist in the next month ready for tour with The Strokes, and I honestly don't know what consequences this will have on a new contract with 4AD. As far as they're concerned, Eternal Youths is all of us. Including you. Without you, I'm not sure where they'll want to go. They might not want to re-sign."

Anthony's heart jumped into his throat. He eyed the other guys, their emotions clearly written on their faces. No one had even contemplated 4AD might not want to re-sign without the entire band. They'd have to find someone as good as Ryan to replace him.

Realizing the dream they'd all worked so fucking hard to achieve was slipping through their fingers, Anthony tried to ignore the other dream that was competing for attention.

Even if they did re-sign with 4AD, they'd only be touring for part of the next year. And they might not even have to do the first tour with The Strokes, only the headliner in the fall.

Anthony swallowed the hope in his throat. If Gideon could have his dream wedding with the love of his life, Anthony might be able to win back the love of his.

39

Julie threw open her building door, trying to not let the day's work wear on her as she stepped into the old elevator. Ruby and Rachel had gone out to lunch, chummy as ever, while Julie was on the phone with a multitude of potential donors. Busying herself with work had helped push aside the loss of Max, the silence with Anthony, the inability to move forward.

She didn't know where to go or what to do, now that she'd lost everything she'd wanted.

And she'd been so close to having it all, too.

The elevator dinged open and Julie tried not to let that thought follow her home, but that's where it resided. She'd been so close to the dream: job, love, family. And then it was just... gone. A terrible decision with consequences she'd seen from a mile away.

Julie stopped in her tracks. Carl's door was ajar, a long lump of clothes holding it open.

"C—Carl?"

She inched forward, noticing the arm splayed out, his shock-white hair sticking out in tufts. Julie dropped to the ground and rolled him over, pulling out her phone at the same time.

Breathe. Breathe. Breathe.

Julie felt a faint pulse on the side of his neck as she gave the address to the 911 dispatcher. His hand was cold in hers while she held it, knelt beside his body. He was wearing his favorite sweater, the last one his late wife had knitted him. Julie tamped down the feeling of what this meant, what it could mean. She'd lost so many people in so many ways.

She was never prepared for any of them.

"Ma'am, I need you to step back."

Julie looked up at the man. She hadn't heard the elevator, or the footsteps of the paramedics.

"S-sorry." She scooted back against the wall, watching as they moved hands over Carl's body, lifting him onto a stretcher.

"Ma'am, do you want to ride with us?" The man knelt beside her.

"Yes. Please."

Julie's feet moved without her being aware, the men in front of her rushing Carl out. She kept up, somehow, climbing into the back of the ambulance. His skin was pale, paler than it should've been, his face unresponsive. His hand never changed temperature.

Julie tried to block out the worried expressions the paramedics wore, the way they stopped working the closer they got to the hospital. She tried to block their panic as they rushed Carl into the ER, everyone shouting codes she only knew from the daytime dramas her mom watched. She stood in the hallway, watching them wheel her neighbor, her friend, through swinging doors marked STAFF ONLY BEYOND THIS POINT.

"Excuse me, ma'am?"

Julie turned to the voice. It sounded more distant than the woman behind the reception desk, but that was the only person staring Julie down.

"Ma'am, are you with the gentleman that just arrived?" The woman shuffled through papers while Julie made her way to the high counter.

"Yeah, Carl — " Julie stopped. She didn't even know what his last name was.

"Carl? Do you have a last name?"

She thought back to all their conversations, all the times she'd stopped at her mailbox right beside his. Julie looked at the nurse and shook her head.

"We're neighbors, I — I found him in his doorway." She fingered the hem of her blouse and shifted her gaze when the nurse glanced at her.

"Any known family?"

"Not that I'm aware of."

"Age? ID? Anything?"

"Not that I'm aware of. I think maybe back at his apartment?"

The nurse sighed. "Okay, I can't finish filling these out until I have more information. Is there someone you can call to bring you his personal effects?"

Julie bit her lower lip. She'd swapped spare apartment keys with Carl a couple months after moving in, for emergencies only. Outside him, only two people had a spare to her apartment. The man she wanted to call was an absolute *no*. Ella was her next choice, but she'd taken the day off work to go to cake tastings with Gideon. Her other friends could probably climb in through the fire escape. Picturing prim-and-proper Rachel shimmying down the fire escape and hauling open an old window almost made Julie chuckle, but then she realized her friend had left early for an event. Ben — she didn't know where Ben was. Julie ran down her list of acquaintances, returning to the one name that scared her.

Anthony.

He'd come. He'd drop everything, she was sure of it. They hadn't spoken since that night, Julie too prideful and Anthony... She'd hurt him enough times. This one was on her to reach out first.

But how did she start? The longer they'd left it, the larger the rift. She'd — they'd — done this so many times, when did it become too much?

"Ma'am, do you have someone you can call?"

Julie looked up at the woman, concern etched in the bags under her eyes.

She nodded. "Yeah, I'll call now. I'll wait for the doctor."

Turning around to the waiting room behind her, she picked a chair in the corner to make her call. They'd been around and around, her and Anthony. And it had become too much. The amount of back and forth they'd been through was ridiculous when, at the heart of it, she'd known one thing: she needed him.

She could only hope he needed her just as much.

40

Washington Square Park was empty, save for the memory Anthony held onto of him and Julie by the arch so many months ago. Max walked beside him, head tilted toward the gray December air, the ringing of Salvation Army donation bells carried on the wind. Anthony needed fresh air and hadn't wanted to be alone. With Gideon out stuffing his face at a wedding cake tasting with the love of his life, and Anthony not trusting Lucas to be in the mood given the drama with Ryan, the only person he could think to wallow with was Max.

He filled Max in on everything that had happened with Julie, and the quiet reassurance from his bandmate was exactly what he needed. He was just sorry it'd taken him so long to really pull Max into the folds of his life.

His phone vibrated in the pocket of his jeans, the name stopping him in his tracks.

Max kept walking while Anthony's heart felt like it was going to leap from his chest. Enough time had passed since they last spoke that Anthony had almost broken down several times and called her first. He felt like the addict he was: always needing to be near her, always wanting her, doing everything required to hear her voice. And every time he felt that urge, he called Gideon. She was the ultimate vice that would undo him. But she'd pushed him around and broke him enough times that he wanted her to feel even an inkling of the pain she'd put him through.

"You good?" Max called out.

"It's her."

Max started walking back, hands in his coat pocket, burrowing his head into his scarf. "Well, pick it up. You've been waiting for this."

Anthony took a deep breath and held the phone to his ear. "Jules?"

"A-Anthony?" Her voice shook, the softness of it threatening to break him.

"Jules, what's wrong?"

She inhaled sharply. "I need you to do me a huge favor. Please. I know we need to talk about... everything. But right now I need you to go to my apartment, get Carl's spare key from the kitchen drawer on the left, the junk drawer, it's green. I need you to go into his apartment, find his wallet, I don't know where it is, and meet me at St. Vincent's on West 12th and 8th Avenue."

"Julie, are you okay? What happened?" Panic seeped into his voice, a stream of potential accidents that could put Julie in the hospital running through his mind.

"Anthony, it's not me. I came home from work a- and Carl... Just, please. I need you."

Something in him snapped, clicked into place.

I need you.

"I'll get there as fast as I can. And Julie? I love you."

He hung up before she could respond and stared at his friend. "I'm sorry man, I need to run an errand for Julie. Thanks for walking with me, it really helped."

"Nah, that's not how this works. Something's wrong, I'm coming with you. Where to?"

Anthony returned his friend's small smile. "This way." He turned on his heel, heading to MacDougal

Street to the south of the park. It was one of those moments that made him believe in something bigger than himself, the fact that he was so close to where she needed him to be. Right time, right place.

Their walk was brisk, silent even, as they hurried up the stairs instead of waiting for the elevator. Anthony stopped at the sight of Carl's open door. Whatever had happened, someone had forgotten to close the door behind them. Anthony sent a silent prayer that Julie lived in a building and an area that was relatively safe.

It was an eerie sight as he carefully stepped into the apartment, Max close on his heels.

The apartment was a mirror to Julie's, only in structure. Where hers had been decorated with modern lines and pops of color, Carl's apartment was cozy. Pictures and artwork covered the warm yellow walls, heavy wood furniture pressed up against almost every inch. Stacks and stacks of boxes, books, old newspapers. The kitchen was the only space he could call clean, but even that was a stretch. The sink was full, the stove covered in stacked pots and pans.

"Ho-llllllly shit," Max said.

"Yeah, no kidding." It came out a whisper as he stepped around Max and toward the coats hanging by the front door. Anthony checked the coat pockets while Max peeked into the bedroom off the kitchen before turning back. The slim leather wallet was cool in his hands, and when he opened it he saw an expired driver's license, one credit card, and a battered fortune cookie.

Your dearest wish will come true.

"Okay, let's go."

"Yes, please." Max shuddered and looked around, inching his way to the front door. "This place reminds me of my grandma's."

"Maybe it's an old person thing. C'mon, let's go."

"Hey, Ant? Do you want me to stay and clean up? If he's in the hospital, and he comes home, someone's going to have to deal with... this." Max turned to look at the dishes, the hoarded memories. "I did it for my grandma, I can do it for Carl."

Anthony looked back at his friend and scanned the room. It might be an invasion of privacy — Carl didn't know Max; hell, Julie hardly knew him — but he was right. And Anthony trusted Max. There was something about the way his eyes dimmed when he mentioned his grandma that reinforced that trust. He was sure Julie would understand.

"Actually, yeah, that'd be great. Thanks, Max."

He gave his friend a slight nod before shutting the door behind him and bounding down the steps.

Right time, right place.

That's always how he'd felt with Julie, and he knew in his bones they would find a way to make it through.

41

The hospital bustled around Julie while she sat in the waiting room, arms crossed in a sad attempt to shield herself. She'd been a guest in the emergency room more times than seemed fair, and she always left with her heart heavy.

Hannah's death.

Anthony's debilitating accident.

Carl, who'd been rushed into surgery.

But an eighty-something-year-old man who collapsed from a cardiac event and was left in the hallway for who knows how long wasn't something that usually bore good news.

Julie glanced at the other people waiting. People. Couples. Families. The weight of her loneliness was something she'd found a way to make peace with, but times like these, she was always reminded how much easier life is with a partner.

So she'd called him. Anthony. Sucking up her pride, she'd called him.

And he'd picked up, waved away their past to make way for their future.

"Jules?"

His voice cut through the din. Julie met his eyes from across the room, a wave of love and apology and relief washing over her. Anthony had come sooner than she expected, but he'd come. He rushed over and fell to his knees before her, hands clasping her face.

"Jules, are you okay?" He felt along her neck, her arms, wide eyes searching her own.

She nodded and pulled him into a hug. "Yeah, yeah. I'm okay."

"Carl? What happened to Carl?"

Julie clung tighter, breathing in his scent. She'd moved past the overt layers of body wash and cologne, finding the musk that she'd always equate to home.

"I found him collapsed in the doorway." She spoke into his neck, fingers digging into his shoulders. "I don't know how long he was there for, and they rushed him into surgery."

Anthony pulled away and reached into his coat pocket. "I'm so sorry, Julie. I found his wallet. Max was with me, he stayed behind to clean up. The apartment was a mess."

Julie took it, the battered brown leather worn smooth soft against her fingers as she turned his words over in her head. She slid his driver's license out of its pocket. Expired. *Carl Townsend*. Born 1940. Finally, her friend had a last name, a birthday. A life. The rest of the contents spoke to what she'd known about Carl — alone, frugal, hopeful. She fingered the fortune and looked at Anthony, the need to kiss him overwhelming.

He smirked and leaned forward until their lips were almost touching.

"You know we have a lot to talk about." His voice was low, hoarse.

"I know."

"You know that no matter what, I'll be there for you."

"I know."

"You know that I love you more than I've ever loved before."

Julie smiled. "I know."

Anthony's lips met hers, soft and gentle. His hands cupped her face as she breathed him in.

"Ms. Milligan?"

Julie pulled away slowly, giving Anthony one last peck before facing what came next.

As long as she had him, she could face anything.

"Ms. Milligan."

Julie looked up, her heart sinking when it was a doctor she faced instead of a nurse. Anthony sat beside her, wrestling her hand from its death grip on the wallet. He cleared his throat.

Then the doctor's voice faded.

Anthony squeezing her shoulder brought her back as the doctor apologized for her loss before leaving.

Julie was used to grief. She was used to how it came up from behind. Sometimes it was a storm, sometimes an ocean. But the numbness sweeping through her veins was new. She'd either kept so busy, so distant, as to not feel anything, or she'd let herself sink and get lost in the emotion. This was her body, her brain, knowing all that was left to do was move forward. Slowly. Deliberately.

She turned to her love, her rock, her life.

"Will you come with me to finish filling out his information? He's an organ donor, I want them to... you know."

"Of course, Julie."

They made their way to the counter, Anthony filling out the paperwork. Julie watched him, his hand gliding across the paper. It never failed to amaze her how someone could be so full of life one moment, but gone the next. Her eyes traveled up his arms, his shoulders, resting on his face. After everything she'd been through — they'd been through — he was the one thing that survived. That stayed.

"Okay, that should be it." Anthony passed the paperwork back to the nurse. "We don't know about any family members or insurance, or if he already made funeral arrangements." He put his arm around Julie's waist and pulled her close, and she leaned against the hard muscles of his body.

"No worries, there is a little time. We — us here at the hospital and yourself — can look into any potential lawyers or family. Depending on the next of kin hierarchy, Mr. Townsend may be left unclaimed unless that's a responsibility you are willing to take. For now, you can go home. We will call you once it's time for next steps."

"Thank you," Julie whispered. She turned, unable to look at the nurse or at Anthony as she made her way out of the hospital.

42

Anthony kept looking over at Julie as they made their way to her apartment building. She'd yet to return his glances, instead keeping her head lowered and hands shoved in her coat pockets.

The first time she'd gone to the hospital, she'd lost her little sister. The last time she'd gone, she almost lost Anthony. He ran his hand through his hair, fingers catching on the ridges leftover from his accident. He shouldn't have survived. Anthony looked at her, his heart breaking with the weight of all her losses.

Somehow, he'd survived. Somehow, he was given another chance.

Julie opened the building door and stopped

short in the lobby. She sighed, her shoulders sagging.

"C'mon, babe," Anthony said gently. He touched her elbow, guiding her to the stairs. He trudged ahead, letting her go as slow as she wanted. At the top of her landing, music filtered from Carl's open door. Anthony smiled at the low hum of Max's voice joining Sarah Vaughan's higher one.

He unlocked Julie's door as she reached the top of the stairs, her glassy eyes staring at Carl's apartment. She smiled at the sound and looked at Anthony, tilting her head to the open door.

Anthony followed her slow steps into the apartment. Max made quick work — the entryway had been cleared, the kitchen cleaned up. The newspapers were probably accounted for in the stuffed trash bags, but the books had been neatly stacked and the dozens of frames dusted.

"Max?" He called out, watching Julie finger the books neatly organized in the living room.

"Yo." Max came from down the hall, stopping when he saw Julie. "Hey, Julie. Can I get you anything?"

"No. Thank you. Anthony told me what you did, thank you so much for... cleaning." She bit her lip and looked around.

Max fiddled with the phone, Vaughan's voice dropping into the background. "Yeah, yeah. Of course. I lived with my grandma so I kinda know what needs to be done. Is... Is he okay?" Anthony caught his eye and shook his head, fingering a hole in his pocket.

"Not really." Julie shuffled to the couch and sank into the threadbare cushion.

"I'm sorry to hear that." Max rested a hand on her shoulder before turning to Anthony. "I'm gonna head out, man. Let me know if there's anything I can do."

"Thanks, Max. Really."

Anthony was taken aback when Max pulled him into a tight hug, but Anthony soon sank into it. Today had shown him how Max was more of a brother than a bandmate, and Anthony welcomed the change to their relationship. He patted Max on the back as he left.

"That was so nice of him." Julie's voice was soft.

Anthony sat beside her, facing her. Out of the hospital and able to really take her in, Julie seemed to shrink to half her size from when he'd last seen her. It'd only been a couple of weeks, but it felt like a lifetime.

"Yeah, he's a really good guy."

She nodded. "He is. But so are you, Anthony. Thank you for coming today."

"Of course, Jules." Anthony couldn't stop a chuckle from escaping. "You know I will always come when you call."

She smiled and looked around. "It's so weird, calling someone a friend when you don't really know them. And now I'll never really know. I had so many questions, but never found the time to just sit and ask him. You know, I didn't even know his last name. Or his birthday. How sad is that?" Her blue eyes were wet when they met Anthony's. "What do you think his wish was?"

"What do you mean?"

"The fortune. In his wallet. It said, '*Your dearest wish will come true.*' What do you think his wish was?"

Anthony remembered the worn slip of paper. It was yellowed from time, creases cutting through the words Carl had held so dear. He looked around the apartment and stopped on the photos. There were some of Carl with a family, the man clearly the patriarch. But there were just as many of Carl with his arm around a man. Anthony could match the Carl in those photos with the Carl in the family photos, following them through the years. But this other man was around for decades, whereas the family photos stopped after the kids had grown.

The realization tumbled through Anthony's brain. His own mom had left her family to start a new one, whereas Carl's family had left him. He thought of all the sacrifices everyone made to make others happy, all the ways people bent and broke to fill the spaces between where they mattered but someone else mattered more.

"I don't know what his dearest wish was, but I know what mine is."

"I know what mine is, too."

He turned to the love of his life, folding a lost blonde lock behind her ear.

She bit her lip before turning to face him.

"Anthony, I want a family. And I want that family with you. I don't know how we'll make it all work, but there has to be a way. And I'm sorry for not telling you everything. I should have, I know. But I was scared. You know, when I was in India someone said something that's really stuck with me: people act either out of love or out of fear. And I'm scared. I'm fucking terrified. But I know that if we're going to make this work, I need to be honest with you about those fears. And I need you to be honest about yours."

Anthony grabbed her hand, so much smaller than his own. "I want you. I want to marry you. I want a family with you. I want a life with you. I was scared by everything, it happened so fast. But I do want what you want. I want us to be able to communicate with each other about it. So if it's fostering, okay. I'm all in, whether it's now or next month or five years from now. My life is with you, whatever that looks like. I'm not going to waste another second."

"Me either. I'm so sorry, Anthony. For everything." Julie threw her arms around his neck.

He held on for dear life, burying his face in her hair. "Me too, Julie."

"Will you move in?" Her throat moved against his shoulder, muffling the words.

"Really?" Anthony laughed and pulled back, smoothing the hair from her face. She laughed and wiped her rosy cheeks.

"I mean, you basically live here anyway. And with the tour next year, I'll basically be living alone."

"Ah, right. The tour," Anthony sighed. It was the one crimp in his perfect plan. Julie hated him being gone for so long, so often.

"Ant, it's okay. I'm in love with you — all of you.

And if you being a famous musician is part of that, so be it. Besides, someone needs to bankroll my life."

He laughed and pulled her into a kiss, tasting the honey of her lips while his hands explored the expanse of her body.

Julie broke away, blushing and panting. "Will you stay over at my place tonight?"

"Always."

43

Julie met Anthony's lips, his magnetic pull easing some of the pain from earlier. And tonight was a night where she wanted to forget the day.

She swung a leg over his until she straddled him, pushing herself as close against him as possible. His hands gripped her ass as he launched them off the couch, carrying her to the building hallway. Julie shut Carl's door behind them as Anthony opened hers, kicking it shut as he continued to devour her mouth.

But instead of taking her to the bedroom, he held onto her even tighter while leaning over the coffee table. Julie heard the thump of books hitting the floor, the crinkle of magazines flying in various directions. Anthony laid her down, the table quietly protesting.

"Um, Anthony…"

"Shh… I need to be inside you. Now."

He knelt over her, careful not to lean too hard on the surface. Julie felt suspended in mid-air, having only the slim wood at her back and the occasional shift of the table's legs as Anthony trailed kisses down her neck. He stopped at the top of her blouse and eased her up enough to peel the fabric from her body. One hand gently pushed her back down while the other went to work on undoing her pants.

They got stuck on her heels coming off, and she laughed. The movement shifted the table, her eyes going wide.

"Two stooges over here," Anthony laughed.

"I wouldn't have it any other way." Julie reached for him, needing to even the discarded-clothing score.

His shirt went flying past her head, his pants soon after.

She craned her neck, her mouth watering at the chiseled god that stood before her. The ache between her thighs deepened. His cock stood at attention, long and thick between his legs, the bobbing head calling to her.

"Please fuck me," Julie whispered.

"Coffee table be damned?" His eyes were dark, need dripping from every word.

"Coffee table be damned."

Anthony leaned over her, fingers sliding through her folds. Gazing into her eyes, he sucked on his fingers, wet with her juices, as his shaft drove into her.

Julie gasped, her body surrendering to the push and pull of his rhythm, forgetting about the sway of the coffee table under their movements. His hands gripped her hips as he thrust into her with abandon. She felt every inch of every hard stroke, the pounding pulling her more and more outside herself. Julie was the ocean, needing to break.

Anthony pushed her legs down towards her torso and angled himself above her. The repositioning sent him even deeper into her body, his grunts and growls growing in ferocity. His fingers tweaked one breast while the other squeezed her thigh, sending her over. The waves crashed as she was thrown into darkness, her voice crying out for him as he pulled out.

44

Before she could gather her bearings, Anthony pulled her off the coffee table and dragged her, stumbling, to the dining table. He folded her over it, relishing the view as his cock found its way home in her dripping sex.

He pumped, the wet slap of his thighs against hers the soundtrack to his need. Anthony eyed her body. He loved the way sweat glistened on her skin, the curve of her spine as her torso stretched across the white table, her perfect peach of an ass high in the air, the hourglass of her curves highlighted while he rammed into her...

He needed to cum, desperately.

But he knew she needed to get fucked into oblivion more.

Julie's moans and stuttered breathing told him to keep going, that she was on the edge again. He ran his hands over her round bottom, the narrow waist, pounding into her without mercy.

She was his.

Anthony needed her to remember that.

Even if he couldn't think beyond the tightening of her muscles around him, the escalation of her cries as his dick was flooded with her release. The wet warmth enveloped him, and he couldn't hold back any longer. He let go. The force of it caused him to jerk, the bliss too splendid and encompassing for him to register anything outside the glow of her body beneath his. Anthony filled her with every part of him, body and soul.

Julie heaved against the table, unsteady as she rested on her elbows. Anthony slid out of her and he grabbed a clean dish towel from the kitchen cabinet to help clean up. She turned around, leaning and panting against the table. Kneeling before her, he guided the cloth over her inner thighs. He gazed up at her. Julie had her head back, her pants slowly turning to deep breaths. Anthony reveled in the glow of the skin of her neck, the curve of her breasts. He loved the way her skin dimpled around her hips, the way her soft belly felt against his scruff as he kissed his way to her lips.

She met him, sweetly, her tongue taking its time as it danced with his. Anthony pulled back. Julie's eyes were closed, a small smile lingering on her face.

"I love you, Anthony Russo. Now take me to bed, I'm tired."

He laughed, burying his face in her neck. Wrapping his arms around her, he breathed her in. "Anything you want."

"You, forever."

"I'm all yours, sunshine."

His hand rested on her neck as he guided her to bed. He ached, but in a hurt-so-good way. The way only really great, hard sex could make him feel. Anthony crawled into bed beside Julie, muscles finally relaxing. He gave his weight to the bed beneath him and caught the weight of his one and only as she fell to sleep.

I will always catch you.

45

Julie's foot trailed its way up the hairy calf, her knee gently nudging the mound that made her weak. She smiled into the chest of the man she loved, grateful for every morning she had to wake up with him.

She peeled herself from his embrace and looked around. Moving boxes stacked in the corner of her bedroom. Dresser drawers that her new roommate always left open. The heady smell of sex dusting the air.

"Good morning, sunshine." The low grumble was followed by fingers trailing down her naked spine. Goose bumps erupted over her skin, and Julie snuggled against Anthony.

"Good morning."

"Ya know, ever since I officially moved in a week

ago, waking up beside you feels different." He kissed her forehead. "I don't think I'll ever get used to it."

Julie pressed against him even more, her ear catching the beat of his heart. "I know what you mean. It's awesome."

"It is awesome." His laugh echoed through his chest before turning into a groan. "Do you know what time it is? I have that band meeting today."

Julie sighed. "Time to get up. I have a meeting today too, Rachel was adamant everyone be in the office today."

"Gross. Meetings."

"I know, right? Adulting." She yawned and swung her legs out of bed, the cold air making her teeth chatter as she made her way to the shower. Leaving a warm bed was hard enough, but even harder when it held a hot sexy man she was madly in love with.

When she entered the living room, drying her air with a towel, a plate of eggs, bacon, and spinach sat on the dining table with a note.

Can't wait to see you later.
Love you forever.

Warmth spread through her body. After they'd cleared the air before filling it with honesty, everything between them had been easy. Right. Like they were exactly where they were supposed to be.

Julie noticed the time and scarfed her breakfast while getting ready for work. She was running a little late, and the slight weight she'd gained had made it impossible to tell which clothes would fit without trying everything on.

By the time she got to the office, everyone else was already seated around the conference table. Julie waved an apology to Rachel and Ella through the glass walls, noticing everyone but Ruby was present. Julie dropped her coat and bag at her desk before joining the crew. Julie sat as Rachel and Ella stood at the front of the room.

"Thanks everyone for making it in today," Rachel started. "It's with a heavy heart we must say Ruby has left her full-time capacity at Maven Media and will be continuing part-time remotely. We won't go into detail, but she was called home and will be there for the foreseeable future."

Ella picked up. "We understand it will be an adjustment. Charlotte, who works with me for our music clients, and Winsome, who works with Rachel for publishing, have offered to help fill in the gaps while we hire an intern to take it on. If you guys have any questions, please let us know."

Ella waited as everyone left the room, but Julie was paralyzed. Ruby had left? Julie knew it didn't mean anything — she and Anthony were better than ever, his fling with Ruby only a distant happening. But not needing to see her every day removed a weight Julie hadn't realized she'd been carrying.

"Jules?" Ella sat on the table beside her, avoiding Julie's gaze. "Sorry I couldn't tell you sooner. It's weird, being friends with... employees."

"El, it's fine. Seriously, I get it. I'm more just, I don't know. In shock? Like, it's a dream come true but now that it's happening I can't believe it's happening."

Ella nodded. "I get that."

"Is — Is everything okay?"

"You know I can't discuss that. How is officially living with Anthony?" Ella playfully kicked Julie's chair.

Julie blushed. "It's perfect. Better than perfect. It feels right, Ella."

"It is right. God knows it took forever for you to get here. This is yours, Jules. I'm so happy for you." Ella scooted off the table and squeezed Julie's shoulder before leaving the room. Julie watched her friend through the window, watched Priya and Rachel, Winsome and Charlotte and Phoebe all at their desks, laughing and talking with each other across the room.

Julie had to admit, it was a little less bright without Ruby. Maybe the intern would have as much grace as Ruby had, and be as forgiving as Julie wish she'd been.

46

The band milled about the rehearsal space, Anthony sitting beside Gideon at the folding table. Max and Lucas were laughing about something. It was their first meeting since Ryan had left, and Anthony felt the absence.

Tom raced into the room.

"Sorry I'm late, guys." He tossed his bag and coat on the table, looking around. "Wow. This is weird."

His words replaced the laughter. Lucas clenched his jaw, Max stared at the ground while Gideon stared at the table. Anthony met his dad's gaze.

Tom cleared his throat. "So good news or bad news first?"

Anthony's heart dropped into his stomach. In unison, the guys agreed to hear the bad news first.

"4AD doesn't want us to open for The Strokes, and they're not sure about re-signing unless we can get the right bassist."

Anthony looked at each of his bandmates, trying to gauge their reaction, but they'd all hung their heads, two of them pacing the room. As disappointing as it was, Anthony couldn't stop the small glimmer of hope that maybe he'd only be gone in the fall of next year, rather than almost the entire year. He fingered the ring in his pocket, the one he'd bought a couple days ago. The ring that was only a symbol for the love he would share with Julie for the rest of their lives.

Gideon sighed. "What's the good news?"

"Good news is, while they don't want us to open for The Strokes, if we find a suitable replacement for Ryan by Monday, we could still perform. It could be a trial run for the newbie. And if we don't find a suitable bassist, we then have a few months before spring to find one to help with the album, which could solidify our chances of being re-signed. And it's possible that if 4AD doesn't want us, another one of the big labels would. Oh, and I have many, many bassists booked for the next week, so I'll need all hands on deck."

A collective groan rose around the room.

"Guys, I vetted them already through demos and interviews. Please, you act like I don't know how to do my job." Tom rolled his eyes.

"Would we want to do a public trial run with the newbie? What if something happens and our rep gets ruined?" Lucas asked.

Max grunted. "Good point, man."

"I think it's too risky," Anthony added. "I'd rather take the time we need to find the right person, and make sure they're a good fit with the band. If we focus on our headliner in the fall, that could really set us up."

"While I agree with Ant, are you sure it's not just so you can spend more time with your fiancée?" Gideon joked, nudging Anthony.

"Fiancée?" Tom asked, his eyes as wide as everyone else's.

"I haven't asked her yet, but we've talked about it. It seems like the right time." Anthony shrugged. He hadn't talked to his dad about it — they were still mending their relationship, and Anthony felt this next step with Julie was something that needed to be just theirs. Gideon probably only knew because Anthony had asked Ella for her blessing and ring guidance, and those two shared everything.

"Congrats, Ant!" Max and Lucas were genuinely

happy, but the hurt leveled at Anthony from Gideon and Tom was hard to bear.

"Thanks, guys. Sorry I didn't say anything sooner, I just needed to clear my head." Anthony looked at his family.

Gideon cleared his throat and stood, speaking to Tom. "So what're we doing today, Hoss?"

"Well, we should go over what we're looking for in our next bassist, and probably go over what we want from the next album. Especially now that we know what rides on it."

Lucas and Max grabbed three more folding chairs from the wall. Anthony went to Gideon. "I'm sorry, Gid. Seriously. It was just something I needed to keep to myself."

"And Ella."

"I needed her help."

"But you had to have known she'd tell me." Gideon looked at his cousin. "I'm honestly just hurt. I get it, I do. But I'm still hurt."

Anthony nodded. "I know. It won't happen again."

Gideon barked out a laugh. "No shit, Sherlock. Come here." He hugged Anthony, a forgiveness in the way he held on a little longer than normal.

Anthony squeezed, forever grateful for the family, the friends, he was surrounded by.

"Love you, man." Gideon's voice cracked. "You deserve this."

Coming from his cousin, those words meant more than anything. Anthony blinked back tears, squeezing his cousin even harder.

47

The bathroom was cold, despite how many laps Julie had paced. She'd chewed through the fresh manicure on her thumb, the box on the sink counter staring at her in all its pink glory. Julie had been so sidetracked with work and Anthony that she hadn't realized her weight gain coincided with being late. And she was never late.

She took a deep breath, hands shaking as she unwrapped the box and pulled out one of the sticks. Two symbols, both of which could be a deciding factor for her future. Julie would be happy with either, but she'd be lying if she said she wasn't nervous about how Anthony felt.

After peeing, the stick sat on the counter and

stared at Julie while she desperately waited for a symbol, any symbol to appear. She froze.

Positive.

Julie did the second test, just to make sure.

Positive.

Feeling light-headed, she placed both hands on the counter and leaned forward. This was it. This was a next step. The next step she'd been wanting her entire life. Julie looked at herself in the mirror, mapping the fine lines on her face that had started slowly appearing over the last year or two. She remembered herself at sixteen, twenty, twenty-five. Nearing thirty, her eyes had grown brighter, her smile wider.

Everything she'd been through had led her to this moment.

The giddiness rose in her belly, climbing its way through her chest until it broke out as a laugh. Julie laughed at the ridiculousness of the journey, the beauty of events, the wonder at this next chapter. She placed one hand on her belly and grabbed the box and used sticks.

Julie hid the box and one stick in one of her dresser drawers, and found an old necklace box for the other stick. Anthony would be home soon, and she wanted to share this gift with him. She wrapped it in some leftover Christmas paper and a black velvet ribbon, setting it at his place at the dining table.

She texted him, asking if he wanted pizza for dinner and if he could pick up some strawberry Häagen-Dazs. Curling up on the couch, she waited for him to come home.

The click of the door opening jolted Julie upright.

"Hey, babe. Were you taking a nap?" Anthony came in, setting the food on the counter and looking at her with surprise.

Julie wiped her face. "Yeah, it was a long day at work. How was your day?"

She put her arms around him, giving him a deep kiss before putting the ice cream away.

"Mmmm, much better now. It was a big day for me as well."

"Well, go get comfy. I'll get plates." Julie gave him a peck and watched him leave. He glanced at the present on the table, a smile playing on his lips as he continued into the bedroom. Julie grabbed cups and plates from the cabinet, asking what he wanted to drink.

Anthony came up behind her and nuzzled her neck. "What's with the present on the table?"

Julie turned to face him. His skin was golden in the dim light, hands behind his back. She eyed him.

"Just a little something. What are you hiding?"

"Just a little something." His eyes twinkled. "Are we having an impromptu gift exchange?"

"That, sir, seems to be the case." Julie laughed, fingering his arms. "Can I open mine first?"

"Of course." Anthony's smile dropped, followed by one knee. A box came forward, the pear diamond bouncing far too much light. Julie gasped, her hand moving to her mouth.

"There will never be words to tell you how I love you, but I have plenty for why. Your compassion, generosity, intelligence. The way you smile — it's the sun on the coldest of days. The way you look at me — no one has ever seen me the way you do. And that's a beautiful thing, to be seen. For the good, the bad, the ugly. No matter how vulnerable I am, you make me feel safe. Through everything, you've seen me. You've pushed me to grow, to be the best version of myself. And I want to give you all that and more for the rest of my life. I promise that even though we will disagree and hurt one another and fight, we will also love and laugh and grow in ways we never thought possible. You are my heart, Juliette Milligan. Will you — "

"Yes!"

Anthony laughed. "I have to finish! Will you marry me?"

"Yes, yes, yes, Anthony Russo. I love you so much." Julie clung to him, showered him in kisses.

He pulled back, placing the large ring on her finger. Julie flexed her hand, unable to believe this was real.

"Can I open mine?" Anthony nibbled her ear, and Julie had to keep from gulping.

"S-sure."

Anthony stalked over to the table, gently shaking the present. Julie had used tissue paper, anticipating Anthony's boyishness when it came to presents. She played with the sleeve of her sweater, suddenly self-conscious about her so-called present. He discarded the ribbon and tore into the paper.

"Aw, babe you know how much I love jewelry," he joked, pulling the lid off.

His face froze, his chest rising and falling a touch faster than before. Julie chewed her lower lip, waiting for him to meet her eyes.

When he did, his smile returned. "Really?" His voice was soft.

Julie nodded. "I took two. I wanted to be sure."

Anthony set the box down and slowly made his way to her. His rough hands cupped her face, and Julie grabbed his wrists. Her thumb rubbed against his heartbeat, finding that it matched her own.

His lips met hers. She swept her tongue around his, gently tasting this man that had given her everything she'd wanted. Everything she'd worked for, deserved, needed. She could feel their love in the way he sank into her. She could see their wedding and their baby and their future in the way he clung to her. She could taste the way he gave her a piece of himself in this kiss, deeper than than any they'd shared.

No matter what happened, this was home.

Thanks so much for reading the Back Stage Series!

Read BREAK ME LIKE A PROMISE: When Ruby Delacey returns to her small town to care for her mom, she's faced with her ex-boyfriend.

Her now-rich, kind-of-an-asshole, still-devastatingly-hot ex-boyfriend.

Her happily ever may be closer to home than she thought — if the man she once abandoned can ever trust her enough to give her second chance.

Click here to read Break Me Like a Promise, the first standalone in the Oak Valley series!

LINKS

Want to receive news first and get exclusive content? Sign up for my newsletter!

Did you enjoy this book? Leave a review and let others know!

Find me online:

Facebook
Instagram
Website

Printed in Great Britain
by Amazon